A
THIRD
STORY

A
THIRD
STORY

by

Carole Taylor

Lace Publications

Library of Congress Cataloging-in-Publication Data

Taylor, Carole, 1947-
A third story.

I. Title.
PS3570.A92718T5   1986   813'.54   86-10306
ISBN 0-917597-06-0

Printed in the United States of America
23456789

Cover design by Lace Publications
Cover illustration by Carole Taylor

Lace Publications
POB 10037
Denver, CO 80210-0037

ISBN 0-917597-06-0

For the Lord, who beamed this to me.

For Mamaw and Mama and Daddy, who taught me to be receptive.

And for Lindy, who convinced me that my pencil could be both antenna and transmitter.

ACKNOWLEDGMENTS

Although writing is ultimately an effort done in solitude, it is not one accomplished in a vacuum. My deepest gratitude goes to these people who provided atmosphere:

Paul and Mary Slaughter for their invaluable critiques and uncommon intelligence. Paul is my Renaissance Man.

Carole Hyndrich for laughing in all the right places and suggesting essential fine tuning.

Ruby Lee Bland and Lorna Shaw for their patience and magic powers over word processors.

Jay Sandrich for his compliments, encouragement and direction.

Hazel Fath for being The White Witch Hazel.

Steve Lucchi, president, and Michael Dreve, vice president of Word Data Corporation, whose CPT word processors and generosity with them saved my sanity.

And Kate Millett who inspired this, even though she doesn't know me and didn't know she did.

Robin Tyler for her encouragement and help to the Memphis equivalent of Adam's house cat!

There are only two or three human stories. And they go on repeating themselves as fiercely as if they had never happened before.

—Willa Cather (1873-1947)

American Author

* * *

Jeanette Harrison decided somewhere around age six that she was not destined to be a ranting, raving beauty. She had good bones but no patience and no artistic talent and thought she couldn't learn how to paint anything, least of all her face. And she preferred wearing glasses to slamming into door facings. Lacking the inclination to barter her face for the socially acceptable form of a steady income, matrimony, she knew she would have to rely on either bluff or brains to produce her fishes and loaves.

Years later, her mother tried to tell her that someday someone would love her for her small, delicate ears. Her mother's oft repeated phrase did not much console Jeanette, as her mother was known neither for her clairvoyance nor her sense of fashion. Besides, having recently discovered the pronouncements of Herr Doctor Freud, Jeanette didn't like the idea of someone loving her for her delicate ears. That seemed sick. She wanted someone to love her for her wit and intelligence. That seemed heresy.

In 1932, Jeanette was only twelve. But she had been aware of her heresy almost since birth, for it was the heresy of her mother carried to its logical conclusion. Her mother had marched with the suffragettes, and when the vote was finally won, couldn't find a job. She fell in love instead, married Mr. Harrison and raised Jeanette at cross purposes: to be a brilliant, inquisitive, versatile girl, whose sole ambition should be to become the assistant manager of yet another nuclear family at a time when

1

this unit was considered a beacon to mankind, as opposed to a group of people who glow in the dark. The attempted inculcation of Mrs. Harrison's lesson in assistant managerhood illustrated the fact that intelligence and wit in a female had only recently been elevated to the status of rumor.

Jeanette loved her father and loved her mother, but of the two, Jeanette and everyone else knew who ran the show. To Jeanette, paternal permission was a myth and resulted in an incredible amount of wasted time traveling from one we'll-see to another. Jeanette even tried improving the efficiency of the decision making process by eliminating her father's contribution to it entirely, only succeeding in adding another round trip.

What did your father say? I didn't ask him. You have to ask him. Ask your mother. She told me to ask you. Well, whatever your mother says. He said to ask you. Tell him yes, but whatever he decides; then come back and let me know.

Jeanette didn't know who had ordained that men should either run everything or take the credit for it, but at twelve she was determined to find out who and get his job. At the time she didn't know that to get his job, she somehow had to look exactly like him or, barring that, hang ill-fitting costumes around her thoughts.

As time and puberty passed, her attitudes became legend, and her drizzle of suitors lost humidity altogether, the resulting arid climate perfect for libraries and study. Volume upon volume of all that men had achieved and destroyed and achieved and destroyed.

It was only logical, to her and her mother at least, that she would pursue a terminal degree and, traveling faster than it ever could, would overtake it.

Terminal. As if it were a disease. But then, in 1948 for a woman, a Ph.D. in history might as well have been herpes.

* * *

It wasn't that the men in her graduate program didn't like Jeanette. They did. It didn't bother them that she was smarter than most of them. They weren't aware of it, because they didn't list her in the same category as themselves; they could ignore her except when it suited them. This process of selective inattention enabled many of them to benefit from her talents without admitting that she had any: She was an extraordinary tutor for her less talented brethren. For free.

They viewed her as a curiosity, not as a competitor. For one thing, she didn't act like a competitor. She shared her ideas, was open and original, and when she scored higher on something, she didn't strut about it.

But what really made her harmless was what they all knew about Jeanette.

What they all knew was that she hadn't a prayer for the jobs they'd be eyeing. They knew that theirs would be the plums of Harvard or Yale or Princeton or some small prestigious New England college like the one in whose halls they now sat. She'd be trying to out-shout eighth grade gonads in some civics class in Kansas.

Not knowing of her classmates' aspirations for her, Jeanette felt little obligation to achieve them. Shortly before graduation, her weighty resumé was postmarked along with those of her esteemed colleagues and came to rest on a president's desk at a university as far from Kansas as Toto.

Long having used her initials as the introduction to her legal signature, she could not be detected on paper as anything but a superior candidate. How she actually got the job became the subject of many a subordinate clause; and the astonished debate, never fully resolved, was finally filed away under pestilence, famine and other acts of God. God, had the question been posed, would probably have accepted blame for two of those acts and credit for one, but wasn't about to reveal which was which.

Jeanette did one other thing before beginning what was to be a long life of scholarship, limited fame as an author of history texts, and celibacy. In 1947 she had an affair with the other woman in her graduating class.

* * *

In the distance two women move slowly through the amber, slanting light of a New England afternoon, through a painting by Degas. Points of light, soft faces, brilliant autumn. Hushed voices in gentle laughter, rustling grasses. A violet and crimson sunset behind a crimson and amber earth. A leather volume of Millay wrapped in ribbons to match the sky. Soft, soft touches, softer smiles.

* * *

Years had passed. Maybe only a day. When she woke on any first morning of autumn, the smell and the feel of the air would consume her as it had forty years ago, and her arms would ache with remembering. But Dr. Harrison would peel her mind from the memory and hang her thoughts instead on sturdier things: her next book to write, or today's students to teach, or that committee, or this project.

She would study everyone's history but her own. She didn't understand her own; she had never discussed it with anyone. Not once. Something which had seemed right at the time, even inevitable, eventually seemed an appalling error in judgment, because she could find no agreement from the one who had shared this particular bit of history with her. History misinterpreted is no history at all, nor is an event witnessed by only one recorder and then erased as fantasy or fallacy. She was alone with her mistake, as she called it to herself. Well, not quite alone, but she didn't know where her friend was. Or now, four decades later, if her friend were even still alive.

Dr. Harrison understood one thing about her mistake: Love conquers nothing. Fear conquers all. The affair had lasted three months; her friend

3

had met a man and married him. For security, she had said. That's not the point, Jeanette. Of course I love you. But I can't *live* with you. You and I—we're not like *that*.

And there was nothing for her to do but agree. Because they *weren't* like *that*. If their mistake had a name, neither of them wanted to know how to spell it.

* * *

Leaning against the dark wood of the window sill, she watches winter begin to drizzle through leafless, lifeless stick trees. Beyond the branches, the Gothic arches of the college hover dark and blurred by the rain. Alone. Drained eyes vacant, Jeanette holds a photograph of herself and her lady. There is no disguising the look in their eyes, the bond between the two minds almost tangible. That look from those eyes. She melts again. Her hands breathe, they sigh apart; the picture tears in half and the pieces drift from her fingers and settle to her desk to lie on the already love-worn leather that binds Edna St. Vincent Millay in truths and intimations.

* * *

Dr. Harrison felt something fuzzy on her hand, then something not quite wet. Lord, she had dozed off. Not like her at all. She opened her eyes and looked over the edge of her bed at her hand and at Dog. Dog dusted the floor twice with her furry mutt's tail and retracted her moist alarm-clock tongue.

"Dog, the truth. It's not my skill with a can opener. It's my delicate ears, isn't it? If only breakfast were *my* sole matter of consequence today."

But Dog knew she was just kidding. At sixty-five, matters of consequence defined Dr. Harrison's life. Passion was an energy to be applied to issues, principles, teaching, study. Her days were arduous, ordered and predictable; and she no longer felt any need to examine her cocoon of consistency. At least not often.

Anyway, this morning there was no time to examine anything but her closet. If she could be said to be indulgent at all, it was in her house and her clothes, but it was an indulgence in good taste. Since she never threw anything away, it was beneficial that her taste ran to styles that survived. She saw no point in throwing away perfectly good clothes simply because they were temporarily out of vogue. Since she stubbornly refused to allow her metabolism to change, she and her size ten figure always managed to wait until fashion completed its orbit and allowed her to resurrect that fine tweed or herringbone or silk. But she was always surprised when people told her she was stylish; she didn't think about it except as a vague realization that she had not aged in the usual ways. Her Katherine Hepburn cheekbones and her walk always in overdrive made her seem ageless. But this morning, as on all mornings, there was not time to consider wrinkles or hemlines.

No time. She always thought there was no time. She actually had an hour to spare, but by her definition, that was late. Dr. Harrison was convinced, as was nearly everyone else, that the University would collapse if their grand dame were ever merely on time.

She launched herself toward her closet doors, dislodging volumes of books from the scholarly walls she built around herself on the bed at night, only room enough among the books and papers for a single, unrestless body.

As she dressed, she reviewed the day's agenda and she thought about today's appointment with Dr. Elizabeth McKay, and then about how she had met Elizabeth eight years before. They had both been tokens on the same committee when Elizabeth had first come to the University. Actually, the entire committee had been a token, the first of several, since it had been ramblingly charged to "investigate possible substantiation of alleged inequities in women's and minorities's salaries at the University and recommend appropriate actions."

"Alleged inequities," Elizabeth had grumbled. "That's like saying 'alleged pregnancy' with a twin already suckling at each breast."

Elizabeth had believed in the beginning that the committee had actually been intended to *do* something. Dr. Harrison had known better. Whatever its stated purpose, however laborious its syntax, the expected result was pure shadow: of no substance and designed to relieve heat.

Their principle, but unavoidable error in creating the committee had been in appointing Dr. Harrison as its chairwoman. No appointment, no task was to her one that was cursory. She was as serious and as focused as a Great White shark with a spare stomach near a fast food beach.

Although the University acted with the blinding speed of oak trees engaged in natural selection, Dr. Harrison believed in the University, natural selection and herself, and that the first and last were inseparable and products of the middle. But she was equally committed to fair play. "Although," she said, "there is an inherent contradiction in the term *fair play*: One ought not trifle with justice."

And concerning the last in a series of "task force" committees, she soothed Elizabeth with, "Charges to committees are like prayers, Kiddle. The supplicant must be positive he wants what he requests. He is likely to get it."

Dr. Harrison smiled over her wirerims at herself as she dressed this morning. Elizabeth made her laugh, made her think, was worthy of being her protegé. She'd been just like her at thirty-two, Elizabeth's age. Well, except that Elizabeth was a beauty, striking, classic. And was practically engaged to Tony Scalla, the best looking man on campus. Or most anywhere.

Tony was a rare animal, not one that would enjoy the jungle but one that could survive in it if necessary. He appreciated, even encouraged Elizabeth's independence. But then Elizabeth would only have selected a rare animal; she had them all around her, thought Dr. Harrison. There's that woman friend of hers, Kincaid Phillips. And me. And as a psychologist, Elizabeth should be a good judge of character.

* * *

The campus mall was virtually empty one moment; the next, scores of doors opened almost simultaneously, releasing long strands of people who snaked across the mall until it became a pit. Moving along a walk, Dr. Harrison was in animated, gesticulating conversation with Elizabeth McKay.

Repeatedly interrupted by students speaking to each of them, the women handled their conversation like verbal athletes, engaging each new player while never losing the ball. Whenever Dr. Harrison was with Elizabeth, she loved to watch people's faces as Elizabeth passed. Nearly everyone, women included, looked as if they'd been given a present or waked to a particularly brilliant sunrise. Or maybe that's what Dr. Harrison saw on their faces because that's what she herself felt. Dr. Harrison saw also that like a sunrise Elizabeth seemed unaware of her effect on people: her dancer's grace and thick auburn hair, her smokey dark eyes and full, intelligent mouth. Actually, it was not at all that Elizabeth wasn't aware; it was that she knew her own history. You couldn't catch Elizabeth without her face on because one of the things that she knew about appearances and reality was that most people didn't think there was a difference. And she remembered that for at least twenty-five of her first years, her thin, athletic grace was out. Short and round were in. So that when her look became desirable, conceit was prevented by memory. Nevertheless, in addition to good bones, Elizabeth had patience and artistic ability, and she used them both to make the already striking canvas of her face into an unforgettable one.

At the moment, Elizabeth's unforgettable face was pinched in frustration over the unreasonable patience Dr. Harrison kept insisting on.

"It's the system, Elizabeth. You've been here long enough to understand it."

"Understanding isn't liking," breathed Elizabeth. "It's ridiculous, Jeanette. They don't *need* another study, another committee, to tell them what they already know: women don't make as much money as men for the same work." Elizabeth sighed in redundant frustration. "You've been a history professor here for thirty years. Women aren't much better off now than when you came here, Jeanette. Certainly not since I started taking notes. And I've been taking notes since I was five. Our only advancement is that there are just more of us being underpaid. Men haven't changed their minds; they just don't announce their opinions anymore."

"You just have to be patient, Elizabeth." Dr. Harrison always became maternal when Elizabeth became frustrated. "To change the system you have to learn it and use it. The alternatives are armed revolt or secession. You don't like violence, and to secede, you have to have somewhere to go. Besides, neither tactic is very original or creative."

"It's amazing to me how creative people can be in maintaining the status quo."

Elizabeth saw Dr. Harrison's eyes crinkle with a dollop of mischief. Dr. Harrison's voice registered almost baritone for her mock pronouncement of truth.

"There's nothing creative about the Three Theses, Elizabeth."

Elizabeth cocked her head, smiling her question. "Three Theses." Dr. Harrison was counting on her fingers, looking as if she were matriculating through scout troops. "How to end any discussion which proposes change. One: We have *always* done it that way. Two: We have *never* done it that way. Or three: It's not in the budget."

"You should have called them the Three Feces. Three Feces and Two Urines."

"Elizabeth!" Dr. Harrison loved to pretend to reprimand Elizabeth, but she always laughed before it was effective.

"You're in the wrong profession because you're insane if you buck the Good Ole Boys." Puns might be the invertebrates of humor, but like escargot Elizabeth couldn't resist them.

"It's aggravating at best, I know, Elizabeth. But we have to go through the motions of doing as we're told, else the Boys might get their feelings hurt." She looked around conspiratorily, then back at Elizabeth. "Men have to think they're in control, Kiddle. Deep in their hearts, they have the sneaking suspicion that we may not need them at all. Thus spake Margaret Mead."

"We need men," said Elizabeth. "But deliver us from Good Ole Boys. Of any age."

They had reached the rear entrance of Dr. Harrison's classroom building, a ponderous, static colonial structure that had been one of the original buildings on the campus. Only because it had housed the president's office at one time had air conditioning and new plumbing been installed. Other than creature comforts, nothing about the building had been altered in a hundred years. Dr. Harrison always used the rear entrance and saw no metaphor in this procedure.

Glancing at her watch, Dr. Harrison started backing toward the door. "You always make me forget the time, Elizabeth. If I don't hurry, the South will secede without me. Don't forget. Dinner at my house. Friday."

"Three hours after World War II? Your version, that is. Not God's."

"Satan's, Kiddle. War was Satan's invention."

Elizabeth watched Dr. Harrison open the door and hold it for several students hugging precarious stacks of books. Dr. Harrison shepherded the students inside and flipped a wave to Elizabeth before the door banged shut.

It was almost as if Elizabeth had been adopted, in an academic sort of way. That Dr. Harrison also treated her as a colleague and friend continued to surprise Elizabeth.

She'd never had a mentor before, and without one, graduate school had been the big cats in the center ring: Jump through this, act ferocious and independent; now the fire, with the promise that at some point the tiger could hold the whip.

Elizabeth wasn't sure she wanted or needed a mentor anyway, since she had no desire to "rise within the system." The phrase for some reason always made her think of vomit.

There seemed no sense in the concept of leaving what you did well and enjoyed in order to fulfill some arbitrary definition of advancement. Her advancement happened in her counseling work with students, seeing the look on their faces when they discovered something about themselves. It fascinated her to watch this growth process, although she only used terms like "growth process" when Tony started to play Very Important Psychologist and to spout the language seemingly invented to provide beaks in a pecking order.

"Let's practice impressing people," he would say, swiveling meaningfully in his office chair, his tongue fastened securely to his cheek.

"Very *good*," she would admire. "The old meaningful analyst's swivel."

"Exacerbate," he would respond.

"Inchoate!" she would exclaim.

"Reciprocal inhibition?" he would speculate.

"Growth process," she would conclude.

"Convolute," he would propose.

Puh-leeze. You had to talk like that all the time and be serious about it to "rise within the system," and she just couldn't sustain the vocabulary with a straight face or a calm stomach. She didn't want to be a promising young administrator or a mid-level manager. She didn't want to manage anything but her own life.

It wasn't an enormous surprise to her that she was an endangered species in this approach to life. Most people felt, if by their fruits one could know them, that they could manage their own lives only by managing everyone else's first. Elizabeth spent considerable energy avoiding these people. She thought they were sick.

Fortunately for her, she wasn't aware at the moment that her path and their fast lane had already crossed.

* * *

Dr. Tony Scalla loved the Lord his God with most of his might because

S/he had blessed him with craggy dimples, dark curly hair and muscles that needed little tending. S/he had also seen fit to introduce him to Elizabeth McKay, the only woman he had ever truly loved.

That was the kind of phrase he would never have said aloud in mixed company, because it was so patently boring. But it was true. He had met Elizabeth soon after he had come to work at the University seven years before, although at the time, they didn't work in the same department. The University underwent so many realignments, shake-downs, lateral moves, reorganizations and 5-year plans which never saw an anniversary, that Tony had worked with everyone remotely connected with psychology. It had been a relief to find Elizabeth, for more reasons that academic.

He and Elizabeth had begun their relationship with an analysis of their shared disdain for the planned chaos around them, thinking somehow that they didn't contribute to it. Like everyone else, they longed for independence. If they could only find a group of like-minded people to support them in their uniqueness. Who would secede with them at precisely the moment they both were ready to leave. Oh, well. Drop back ten and punt. But lacking all else, Tony liked his work for a variety of reasons, not the least of which was that he did it next door to Elizabeth.

It helped their relationship that they had such things in common as age, job, tastes, education and world view. But what he liked best about their relationship was that Elizabeth refused to marry him or even have his children. Yet everyone thought of them as joined at the shoulders. Some, he knew, relished the thought of them joined at the sternum, but there were sickies in every crowd. Tony knew the term "sick" was prejudicial and bigoted and he rarely used it publicly. He also knew his private definition of it and that his was accurate. In this certainty, he was neither alone nor correct.

Tony was relieved that his clients didn't include sick people. The students he saw weren't sick, they just "used inadequate or inappropriate coping mechanisms." At least that's what his new boss, Dr. Fred Curtis, would have called it when he wanted to sound informed. Or if Curtis had known where to look it up in order to say it at all.

A year ago, Tony, Elizabeth and the other psychologist on staff, David Stein, had all been rubble in the University's most recent administrative Vesuvius. After all the rumblings, voluminous belches of hot air and rifts in the structure, the latest reorganization had bestowed on their department one Dr. Fred Curtis as its new, albeit befuddled, head.

Tony avoided Curtis whenever humanly possible, this not being exceptionally difficult since Tony didn't consider Curtis human. Tony had work to do, and it didn't facilitate anything for Curtis not to know desensitization from Shinola.

"The least they could have done was give us someone with a degree in our field," Tony had fumed to David and Elizabeth as they congregated around the as-yet-unpaid-for Xerox Machine. "Educational Administration. Please. The terms are mutually exclusive. Like military intelligence."

"It's your own fault, Tony," said Elizabeth. "You could have applied for the position yourself."

Tony raised his nose and looked down it at them teasingly. "I have a reasonable form of acrophobia: fear of hierarchy."

David toyed with the Semetic emblem hanging on a chain around his neck. "You would have been a poor choice, anyway," he kidded. "Assistant Dean for Student Conduct and Discipline? You have no qualifications. None."

"*Au contraire*! It's not what you know or whom you know, but what you know on whom," said Tony, more knowingly than he knew.

David snorted at that. He didn't like that game and knew that Tony and Elizabeth liked it even less. But the difference between Elizabeth and both of them was that Elizabeth couldn't go into the locker room.

Another part of the game was wearing the right color uniform so you could spot and be spotted by the enemy. According to the game as currently played, one dressed in the appropriate uniform, a dark suit and tie, since it required little thought and less time than it did to deal with the repercussions of exercising the freedoms of expression and assembly. If you dressed like one of the students and hung around with them more than was "professionally" required, you were liable to be treated like one of them.

Whatever had been learned in the student upheavals of the sixties had been promptly forgotten by nearly everyone. Forgotten or ignored. David Stein hadn't forgotten them, since he was a retired radical himself. But he couldn't feed a wife and two kids and visit his parents in Miami twice a year by carrying slogans around. At least that's what Elizabeth said, and she knew better than he.

David and his wife Kathy had known Tony and Elizabeth for years, and the Steins were among the few people at the University who really knew anything about Tony's real relationship with Elizabeth. It was more complicated than seemed evident to everyone else, and it had taken a lot of patience on David's part before Tony or Elizabeth had felt close enough to him to explain it. Patience was David's strength, which his mother said was a good thing for a Jewish boy to have. He had a feeling patience was something they'd all need with Fred Curtis being flailed about by the helm of his new appointment.

* * *

Fred Curtis was inordinately pleased with himself. He was so adept, in fact, at being pleased with himself that he could accomplish the feeling while having little or no basis for it. He thus avoided spending much time entertaining the possibility that he wasn't very bright. Both his age and his girth clamored down the steep side of 50, and more often than not, so did his social I.Q.

He had made a few mistakes in his seventeen years at the University. But not big ones. Not the kind you couldn't lay at someone else's door. Or call a buddy to go to bat for you. Curtis had buddies all over campus because he had worked all over campus. Every time there was a reorganization, an event which occurred as soon as a maximum of twelve people were familiar with the intricacies of the last shuffle, Curtis bounced or ricocheted into another department. He tried to view these moves as promotions. No one else possessed a telescope of that magnitude; but it didn't matter. *He* knew. Curtis knew he was blessed with a number of talents, even though frequently frustrated in his attempts to make his supervisors see them. Didn't matter. *He* knew.

For one thing, Curtis knew how to press flesh. All through school his father had said Fred should go into politics. And he had. That is, years ago he had tried to. He had tried to run for the School Board two or three times. It wasn't his fault that no one seemed to agree that improving elementary intramurals was number one priority for the city schools.

Didn't matter. *He* knew. But he had given up running for public office and concentrated on his career in education. Long ago his wife had told him that his only chance for advancement was to finish a doctoral program, and had it not been for her, he could never have gotten that abbreviated prefix that insinuated intelligence. His wife, whom he'd married twenty-five years before, supported him in all his ambitions. She had written and typed most of his papers in graduate school. He showed his gratitude by giving her two sons to raise between assignments. His sons were his pride and almost joy, for both of them were talented athletes despite his years of coaching them. He had given up looking for a coaching job when a spot at the University had come up. Nevertheless, that's what he always wanted to be: a coach. Because that was his other talent: spotting talent. He didn't know what to do with it once he had it, but he could spot it.

That was why, today, he was inordinately pleased with himself. He had just spotted and hired Chuck Gardner, the talented twenty-nine year old son of the University's most important alumni. Which couldn't help but put a little polish on Curtis' career. And his career, at present, was in need of a little chamois cloth. Old man Gardner's boy had just been installed as chief buffer.

Another of Fred's talents: doing favors. He never turned down a opportunity and only called in his own markers when his pride or his job was at stake. He tried not to think about how frequently or how recently both emergencies had arisen.

Curtis ran his hand through his thinning hair and glanced around his office while he tried to think of an astute observation to make to Chuck. Although Curtis had moved into his office over a year ago, he still hadn't finished unpacking. Even if he had, he didn't have enough books to fill the shelves behind his desk, and the lonely, sad little clumps of books looked orphaned. His wife needed to do something to brighten the place up for him. Even his philodendron was nearly dead. His wife had told him to get rid of it anyway, because in her voracious reading she had discovered the maxim that philodendrons were never found in important people's offices. Important people had expensive, temperamental foliage that proved that the owners could afford both the plants and a nanny who could be compelled to fuss over them.

Curtis looked up and saw Chuck's slate eyes watching him and Curtis realized he had said nothing for several seconds.

"Let me repeat, reiterate and say again," resaid Curtis, "how pleased we are to have you on board, Chuck." Curtis smiled at his command of the situation and the language. "When Dr. Thompson said you were looking for a post, I was afraid we couldn't juggle the budget enough to fit you in here. But you and your father know Paul Thompson. Where there's a will . . ."

Where there's a will, there's an inheritance, thought Chuck, smiling at this latest of his relatively uninterrupted successes. Dr. Paul Thompson owed him one, or actually owed his father several, and was the most powerful man on campus because he controlled and tracked every dollar that came to the school and was responsible for the geometric growth of contributions from people like Chuck's father. Chuck's father not only gave sizable amounts to the school's endowment, but also was responsible for other waves of money that flowed behind him in his wake. So Dr. Thompson owed Chuck's father and this job was the first installment. Chuck had been promised the inside lane. But only if he proved himself. That was his father's unremitting requirement. You couldn't be quarterback just because you were the coach's son. But his daddy wasn't the coach. His daddy had paid for the field house. And the field itself.

Chuck's train of thought was derailed by Curtis' rambling redundancies.

"—of course and without question," Curtis blathered. It was obvious, even to Curtis, that he didn't know what he'd been talking about himself, so Chuck didn't feel required to respond.

Curtis cleared his throat in lieu of something less profound and pushed his chair back. He had read somewhere that this would signal the end of a business conversation, and that subordinates would then know to leave without being asked.

Football practice was beginning on the field beyond his office window, and he wanted to watch. Alone, he could pretend he was the coach. Sometimes, one of the players.

Curtis smiled as Chuck closed the door behind him, and he turned to watch the team trot onto the field. Finally he had someone he could talk to on his staff, someone he could have a beer with, go fishing with. Not like

12

the rest of these people. David Stein was a Jew. Good at his job, but a Jew nonetheless. Tony Scalla. Scalla was, well, there was something about the man he didn't like. Probably that he was so good-looking it made Curtis uncomfortable somehow. Besides, he could tell Tony didn't like him. And Elizabeth. Well, you couldn't go fishing with a woman.

Chuck could be like a son to him. He sighed. He didn't seem to have much in common with his own grown sons anymore. He couldn't afford to send them away to school. But he wouldn't have let them go to another school even if he'd had the money. The only perk he had earned for staying here almost two decades was free tuition for his kids. Neither of his two sons was doing very well in their chosen fields of study since neither was clear what his field was, other than possibly wild oat. He tried to encourage them both, particularly Fred Junior, the one that had made first string tight end this fall. But they didn't seem to talk anymore without the last sentence being punctuated by a slammed door. Had he thought about it, Curtis might have discovered that slammed doors were the most frequent event in his life.

He looked out the window and saw his son sitting on the sidelines of the practice field. Curtis couldn't hear them, but outside he suspected signals were being called.

* * *

"What do you have against him, Lizbuth?"

Curtis was smiling paternally at Elizabeth, which was the only way he ever smiled at her. He thought she was incredibly attractive, but her intelligence confused him. Feeling paternal removed the anxiety that other more obvious reactions might have caused.

Elizabeth sighed and leaned back in the chair across from his desk on which rested the worn soles of his propped-up shoes. He was missing, as usual, both the point and the pronunciation of her name. Elizabeth looked at the worn soles and wondered about the essence of a man who felt it necessary to wear a striped tie on the same day he wore these screaming plaid pants, no two colors of which were repeated anywhere except in the leaves of his dying philodendron. She also wondered whether his wife allowed or encouraged him to leave the house that way. She looked at him and sighed again.

"I don't have anything against Chuck, Fred. I don't have anything against you either." Her voice was measured. "But what you've done, Fred, is illegal. Not to mention unfair."

Curtis knew how to handle this one; he'd had lots of training at home and on the job. No problem. He patted her chidingly on her head with his cheshire voice.

"Now, Lizbuth. You're taking this thing too seriously. Too personally. It's only money. You know your work is vital here."

"So vital it's worth four thousand a year less than Chuck's work. He's been here exactly two weeks and three days. A Ph.D. like me. And *zero* experience." She hated dealing with Curtis. She always left meetings with him almost certain he had shipped his brain to Pittsburgh two days earlier.

Curtis looked for an instant as if something made sense; his eyes followed it, but he blinked, and it was gone. He tried to restate his cause to the patch of air above her head.

"It's not that Chuck Gardner is worth more than you, Lizbuth. It's, well, just that we had to pay him more."

Pittsburgh, she thought. "Somehow, I fail to see the distinction." Her patience was spinning out like twine suspending an elephant.

"Starting salaries aren't what they used to be, Lizbuth." Curtis had clicked his vocal chords into administrative gear, and he began to drone smoothly down what he hoped was the inside track. "The market goes up, we have to go up with it. Inflation, you know."

Elizabeth's eyes said she wasn't buying this load. And precisely because he had nothing left to say, he felt he needed to continue. "The University would go broke if we adjusted everyone's salary. We can't afford to be completely equitable."

Raising his hands in a gesture intended to suggest helplessness, he pushed his chair away from his desk. She didn't budge.

"Lizbuth, believe me. I want to help you. But there's nothing I can do. The money's not in the budget. My hands are tied."

Elizabeth's eyes narrowed slightly.

"Fred," she said, punctuating each word with an infinitesimal pause, "you know that I know that that is an evasion. You submitted the budget."

He hated having to explain something he really didn't understand. Besides, it wasn't his fault. His budget was too small before he'd been told to hire Chuck Gardner. They hadn't given him the money he'd asked for to begin with.

"They didn't give me the money I asked for," he said terminally.

"That's not news. They never do." She was trying to keep the anger and frustration out of her voice. "But they let you add a position when precious few were added anywhere."

She failed. He heard it anyway. Now thoroughly threatened, he gathered the stole of authority around his squaring shoulders and stood.

"I wasn't aware that we needed your approval to hire another psychologist, Lizbuth." Sure again of his position in life, he felt fatherly once more and softened his tone to a reprimand. "What you need, dear, is a little more speed-a-court."

Elizabeth dropped her eyes, not under the weight of the reprimand but to keep her face from cracking at his insistence on maiming yet another language. *Espirit de corps.* She had become adept at translating Curtisian phrases. Sometimes it was all she and Tony and David could do to get through a staff meeting without blowing out at least one sinus cavity with an ill-timed sip of coffee.

"Fred, look," she said, quietly trying again to make her point, "I have a lawyer. She says I have a strong case; that I will win if I file suit."

She took a breath, watching his face. "I don't want to sue. I want to solve it here. I'd like an answer by Monday. In writing."

His left eye twitched slightly and the muscles around his chin tightened. "That sounded like a threat, Lizbuth. The University doesn't like to be threatened."

"This isn't a threat, Fred," she said, rising and moving to the door. "This is fair warning." She looked at him one long second, both with regret and insistence and stepped into the hall, closing the door behind her.

She hadn't expected it to be easy. When anyone challenged Curtis' decision on anything, he shifted his pronouns. To the dictatorial They or the royal We. In one case he was just checking chevrons and following orders; in the other, he levitated himself to keeper of state secrets and traditions. Within plural pronouns he was no longer alone in his logic. Or lack of it.

* * *

He slumped into his chair, feeling alone, focusing on the door Elizabeth had just shut. His chair springs groused under his ample weight as Curtis rocked back and swiveled himself around to face his near-barren bookcase. Finding no help there, he whirled back to face his desk and brought his fist down sharply next to his phone and intercom.

He punched the button on his intercom and waited as he massaged his injured hand. "Martha, get Sam Fitzhugh on the line, will ya? In the legal office."

He saw a button flash on his phone and waited for Martha to respond. Leaning back impatiently, he propped his feet on the desk, knocking over a coffee cup filled with ballpoints that had ceased cooperating years ago.

The intercom breathed with Martha's crispness. "Dr. C., Mr. Fitzhugh's secreta—"

"Got it, Martha. Got it." He cut her off and hit his phone button simultaneously. His lips lit with a close facsimile of his drinking-buddy smile.

"Hey, Sam, you old shitface—"

His lips froze and his eyes glazed for an instant. As his ears developed a magenta tint, the smile melted, first into blank surprise, then dripped into embarrassment.

"Oh, Sally. I thought Sam was on the . . . Yes, I'll hold."

Punching the intercom angrily, he ground out, "Martha. Would it be too much to ask for you to tell me *who* is on the phone. You got his secretary. Not Fitzhugh."

Without waiting for a response, he snapped the intercom off with a preemptory jerk of his arm.

"Jesus. Everybody's trying to make me look like an idiot."

His smile didn't return.

"Sam? Fred Curtis. Yeah, fine. Look, I think we may have a problem here. Well, not a problem, really. A concern, maybe. Possibly a wrinkle." He sat up sharply. "No, no. Not here. *Your* office. About two? Yeah. See you then."

* * *

Elizabeth had studied psychology because she wanted to understand herself. And also because when she was listening to someone else she didn't think about her own problems. Most people couldn't imagine that she could ever have had any problems, but that was because she was a very private person and didn't share her life with anyone until she had scrutinized them intensely. That's why she had never married. Under scrutiny the men she had met had revealed that they held an unrealistically high opinion of themselves, one that required for its support the view that she, and other women were lesser beings. She felt that measurement was helpful only in such things as recipes, maps and football; but that concepts such as bigger, better, winning and losing were less helpful in human relations. *Different* was the term she preferred. She had yet to meet a man, even Tony whom she loved better than any of them, that didn't retain a vestige of the feeling of superiority, however small. Most of the time she could avoid people like that socially, but in a work situation the conflict was inevitable. She didn't know of a single organization that didn't have as one of its cardinal sins and grounds for immediate termination the infinite acts of insubordination. She thought the writers of these rules of conduct at best ignorant of human nature, if not ignorant of human essence and the inevitability of expression itself. People were *never* subordinate; they just learned to be silent.

Elizabeth hadn't learned silence too well because her parents had always encouraged debate and her teachers had been for the most part impressed by her ability. Since she had always been first in her class, if not in the whole school and a leader besides, it came as a real shock to her after graduate school that men were supposed to be smarter and stronger than she. Since they had not been previously, that seemed an odd turn of events, if not a rewriting of history altogether.

Today, Fred Curtis seemed to have expanded his skill for revision and was using it to ignore her contribution to the department as well as the time she'd put in.

Elizabeth could never be sure what Curtis' motives were or even if he had any. Well, that wasn't fair. He was doing the best he could. Elizabeth just wished he were doing it somewhere else.

16

The problem was he tried to please everybody and thought everybody should be content with the intention, never mind about the result. Or maybe he didn't want to displease anyone, which was a hair's difference.

Convoluted. That's how she always got when she tried to understand Fred.

She pulled herself back into the present and tried to concentrate on the therapy session she was conducting in her office and on the problems of the student in front of her.

Lisa Hunter was a very tall, pretty twenty-one year old junior at the University, and like most people her age, she was trying to solve all those original, antique dilemmas about personal taxonomy and geography.

Who am I, where am I and where am I going were in Tony's list along with convolute and growth process. The jargon might be good for a laugh, but the situations they describe never were.

Lisa was in pain and trying to avoid it. She stalled a lot in these sessions, and she was stalling again. She hadn't come in here to talk about Nita. That friendship was dead and gone. But here the topic always seemed to come up. Maybe because it hurt so much. Lisa hadn't told Elizabeth everything about Nita and didn't think she would. She liked spending time with Elizabeth and sometimes even invented reasons to see her more than once a week.

Lisa avoided Elizabeth's eyes most of the time, felt transparent when Elizabeth looked at her. She felt transparent now.

"Nita was my best friend. *Best* friend," Lisa's voice bordered on pleading. She stopped and looked away. "I knew her better than anyone knew her, even her boyfriend. Husband, now."

Elizabeth listened hard. Was that resentment, that little break in her voice?

"When she got married, Nita asked me to *serve* at her wedding. Not be *in* it, a part of it. Just serve the damn punch." Her green eyes focused on a dust mote near the window, and she worried the inside of her lip between her teeth.

Elizabeth waited.

Lisa had the contents of the office memorized, but her eyes wandered around it again. The only thing the room lacked was a fireplace or maybe a stove. Plants and books were everywhere. Big, comfortable wingback chairs. Occasional chairs, she thought. She and Nita had loved to laugh about phrases like occasional chairs and part-time people.

"Do they become tables sometimes, as the mood strikes?" Nita would snort. They were always laughing. Like Dr. McKay and Dr. Scalla in the photograph there on the desk. Or Dr. McKay and the other pretty woman in that larger snapshot.

"How do you feel about Nita now, Lisa? How do you feel about what happened?"

Lisa was staring at the framed posters hanging across from her. One was a picture of a B-1 bomber that looked like it belonged in a recruiting office. But in small letters across the bottom it said, "It'll be a great day when our schools get all the money they need, and the Air Force has to hold a bake sale to buy a bomber." Next to it was a picture of a wilting rose with a message: "It's not that God doesn't answer all our prayers. It's just that sometimes S/he says no."

Lisa took a deep breath and rolled her head around slowly to pop her neck, her golden hair rearranging itself.

"I feel like I didn't exist," sighed Lisa. "And that my feelings don't matter. Now, I just feel alone. Different."

"I hear you saying that feeling different feels bad," Elizabeth said quietly.

Lisa looked at her with impatience.

"It felt bad last week, didn't it? It *still* feels bad." She wiped her hands on her faded, skin-tight jeans and looked away. "When are we going to *get* somewhere with this? Are we in an echo chamber? Don't you have anything *new* to say?"

Elizabeth looked at her calmly, almost quizzically. "Don't you?"

"I'm *sorry*," Lisa flared. "I'm fresh out of new problems this week. Sorry I'm not more inventive for you. You don't seem to have any new solutions either."

"You have the solutions, Lisa. I don't."

"Then what the hell am I doing here?"

"I don't know, Lisa. Why *are* you here?"

"Because I thought you'd . . . understand."

"Understanding I can give you. Solutions you provide yourself."

Lisa gave an ironic little snort. "I can't even come up with the right questions."

She looked around again at the bits and pieces of Elizabeth's life that hung on the walls and that lounged on the shelves. Two master's degrees: history and psychology. Ph.D.: psychology. Board of Directors: Symphony. Honey: Dr. Tony Scalla. Life: in order, on track. It was obvious to anyone who saw her office that Elizabeth was a budding bulwark of society, everything that Lisa wanted to become. But the distance between them seemed light years to Lisa.

"How could you understand, anyway?" Angrily, Lisa waved her arm to include the contents of Elizabeth's office. "We're too different. Look who you are, who I am. You can't understand me."

"I might if you *tell* me, Lisa. Stop playing Guess What I'm Thinking. I don't have time for that. Neither do you."

Lisa stared stubbornly at Elizabeth a moment then looked away and clinched her eyes shut. When she spoke, her voice was tiny, adrift.

"Please . . . I don't have anyone else to talk to. I need . . . to see you."

18

Elizabeth leaned forward and touched Lisa's arm. "You can, Lisa," she said softly. "That's not the point. You want *me* to do all the work."

Lisa felt Elizabeth's fingers on her arm, and she blinked under the soft weight of them, her jaw tightening. With conscious effort, she held herself still. Then she folded her arms and turned her body slightly away. Elizabeth withdrew her hand and sat back, waiting.

Finally Lisa sighed and scooted further down in her chair.

"You're the one who's not fair," Lisa said softly. "I can't even stay mad at you. I thought anger was supposed to be therapeutic."

"Sometimes. Something else usually comes first. Fear. Or hurt." Elizabeth paused a second. "So, Lisa. Which is it? Are you hurt or scared?"

"Neither!" Lisa's eyes darted defensively.

Elizabeth rubbed her forehead tiredly, then reached for a folder on the table next to her. "All right. Fine. I'll work on this report. You can collect dust till your time's up." She opened the folder and picked up a pen.

A frown settled onto Lisa's face as she hesitated, then sighed heavily.

"No, come on. Please. You just seemed . . . preoccupied when we started." Her voice and eyes dropped, embarrassed. "I wanted your attention. My feelings were hurt."

Elizabeth blinked and cocked her head slightly, kicking herself with a mental toe. "You're right, Lisa. I'm sorry. I shouldn't have let anything intrude on your time."

Looking up quickly, Lisa started shaking her head. "Oh no, no, Dr. McKay, it was me. I'm sorry. I shouldn't be so . . . so childish, so fragile."

"*I* messed up, Lisa. Let *me* apologize."

Lisa's mouth was still open for further protest. She closed it, her lips making a sheepish pout. "I do that a lot, huh?"

"You don't need to do it here," said Elizabeth gently. "Feeling hurt doesn't mean you're childish *or* fragile." Putting the folder aside, she leaned back in her chair. "The feelings, Lisa. Tell me about them."

Lisa breathed softly, looking relieved. Scooting further down in her chair, she dropped her head back and began searching for her feelings in the light fixture.

* * *

Martha Huddleston loved to laugh. Other than sex with her husband, she couldn't think of anything she'd rather do. And a good laugh could get you through most anything, whereas you couldn't always say the same for sex. Plus, laughing you could do in public and even when you got real old and feeble.

It was because she liked to enjoy herself that she was so good at her job. Whatever she had to do, she did it as fast and as accurately as possible so she could play. And as the receptionist/secretary/bookkeeper/gofer/ diplomat for the University's Student Counseling Center, she spent most of the day trying to find something entertaining about the task in front of her. Dealing with her tasks without good humor allowed only one alternative: felonious assault.

Trouble. That's all that ever darkened her door.

This new white guy that Fred had hired was turning out to be more trouble than Fred. A specialist in testing and measurement, Fred had said. He sure is, Martha thought. He's testing my patience and measuring my ability to read hieroglyphics. She couldn't see how in the world Chuck had ever gotten out of the second grade, much less graduate school. He must have done it on good looks, because you sure as hell couldn't read this rooster-scratching he called a report.

Oh, sweet Jesus. And there he comes now, in all his radiant blond haired, muscled glory. Dr. Gardner, that is. She tightened her jaw. She almost would have preferred seeing Jesus to this particular lower case second coming: Chuck had already asked for his report once that day.

For some odd and unexamined reason, Chuck was as proud of his illegible handwriting as he was of his gene pool. Probably because it was a product of his gene pool. All the men in his family had been successful, handsome, intelligent, powerful and illegible. Actually, it hurt his feelings when someone didn't understand that those characteristics were inseparable, and then demonstrated their insensitivity by not being able to read his writing. He didn't realize his feelings were hurt; he only realized that is pissed him off.

Right now, he was pissed at Martha, and he silently attributed her insensitivity to her own gene pool, originating as it had generations ago in Ethiopia. Looking over her shoulder, he saw she was only on page three. At this rate, he'd get it back by Christmas. But what year?

He was about to ask her what year when he heard Elizabeth's door open. Lisa Hunter was backing out the door and smiling at Elizabeth.

"You always make me feel better."

"You deserve the credit for that, Lisa. Friday, don't forget." Elizabeth leaned against the door frame with one leg bent. Chuck was following the line of her thigh upward when it was removed from his sight by Lisa's Calvin Kleined bottom.

Slightly surprised by Lisa's awkward hug, Elizabeth returned it briefly. Turning to go, Lisa looked up and saw Chuck's eyes following her, reading her. Her smile left before she did.

Elizabeth walked over to Martha's desk and picked up a stack of mail Martha had sorted for her. All of Martha's other four bosses asked her to deliver their mail to their desks. Elizabeth said she didn't want to be waited on. Besides, she came right by there fifty times a day anyway.

Chuck looked at Elizabeth. "That was Lisa Hunter." A statement. As if he thought Elizabeth might possibly have talked to someone, a client, for an hour without knowing her name.

20

Elizabeth slapped her forehead. "That's *it*! I *thought* I knew that girl from somewhere." She was smiling teasingly. He wasn't. Martha covered her mouth and looked constipated.

Sometimes her timing was off. But then, some people just didn't think she was funny. Some people didn't think anything was. Elizabeth thought perhaps Chuck was one of them. Maybe he was just having a bad day. She certainly was.

Martha was a master of self-control, deference and diversionary tactics. "Dr. Gardner," she said, "could you have the steno pool do a draft for me? I'm sorry, but I'm not used to your handwriting yet. I could use the draft as my Rosetta Stone to crack the code, so to speak."

Chuck ignored her, speaking authoritatively instead to Elizabeth. "I'd like to discuss something with you. I've been reviewing it this morning."

Elizabeth didn't like authoritative tones of voice, not even her own, and she was sure it showed in her eyes. But she blinked it away, nodded and turned toward her door.

"No," he said, "my office. The material's there." He had already turned and was sauntering down the hall.

Elizabeth glanced at Martha and saw the residue of Chuck's snub still swirling in Martha's eyes. He evidently doesn't know who runs this place, Elizabeth thought, looking at Martha's angry black face. Else he'd be more careful with her.

Elizabeth gave a little shrug to diffuse Martha's anger and turned to walk behind Chuck, suddenly in step and precisely imitating his swagger, knowing Martha needed a laugh. The instant his head started to turn toward her, she jerked into her own fluid walk. Glancing momentarily at her, he opened his door and went in. Elizabeth paused and looked back at Martha, who was already holding her hand over her mouth and snorting. Dragging one finger across her forehead, Elizabeth hung her tongue out at Martha and wiped imaginary sweaty relief from her brow.

Girl, you're verging. Gonna get caught one of these days, Martha thought, looking at Elizabeth's back, then down at her typewriter. She reached for the half-finished page three and pulled it slowly from the carriage. Holding the sheet by one corner as if it were a soiled diaper, she dropped it distastefully into her trashcan. She reached across her desk for the top folder in a six inch stack of work and cracked her knuckles as Elizabeth closed Chuck's door.

Within days after Chuck's arrival at the University, he had imposed on his office a decor which seemed to Elizabeth both expensive and chilly. He had moved everything out that belonged to the school and replaced it with wall-to-wall chrome and glass, scores of statistics and mathematics texts and a pipe rack, although she had never seen him smoke any of the pipes. There were no photographs of family or friends, and the only truly personal items in the room were a number of collegiate sports trophies placed so that no matter where a person sat or stood, Chuck's name was at eye level.

The furniture was very high tech and Chuck was very high prep. Not Elizabeth's type at all, but she was sure his fine, square features would appeal to any number of her friends.

"I think I have some insights for you on that Hunter girl," Chuck said in a superior tone. Who knew, she thought. Maybe it was his larynx, not his attitude.

Elizabeth's eyes narrowed by a hair, studying him. "What about her?" She was trying to keep the edge out of her voice.

Chuck handed her a folder from his desk. "Her intake tests are interesting, and the interpretation is particularly complicated here. Thought I could help you with it." It was not his larynx.

That tacky beast sarcasm was beating its nasty little fists against her lips, begging to be free. She tried to contain it.

"Thank you. I wonder what I missed when I went over those again last week."

Chuck hesitated an instant, thinking he heard something in her voice. Maybe not. "Look at this," he said, pointing to papers in his folder. "And here. And this response."

Elizabeth read each thing he pointed to, although she knew it by heart. While she read, he had a chance to look between the buttons of her blouse. Finally, she looked up and saw where his eyes made silent forays. If she hadn't already been stressed, she might have taken it as a compliment, if that's how he'd intended it. Now it only made her flex her jaw and stare silently at him.

One of them was missing a verb, and he was certain it was Elizabeth.

"Well?" he said.

"I studied these last month. And a week ago. I don't see anything new."

Chuck pointed impatiently to the folder. "It's obvious to me. Look at this page."

Watching his face and not the page, she sat on the arm of one of his chairs. He sighed and took the folder from her. It drove him crazy when people made him explain what for him was obvious.

"I was right," he said. "You do need help. You evidently can't see that the girl has tendencies." He waited again for a response. Nothing.

He took a deep breath and let it out before saying with emphatic separation, "Lesbian . . . tendencies."

Elizabeth still just sat there watching his eyes, something between impatience and pity in hers. It reminded him of his mother's look when he expected her to find something for him that he himself had carelessly misplaced.

"That's a very complex conclusion," she said quietly. "Has she talked with you?"

"No."

"Just the tests."

"And I've watched her. She has difficulty relating to the men in the office." He turned and sat posing on the edge of his desk. "Even me."

He waited pointlessly for her to respond. He had no doubt that he knew what he was talking about here. In college, a fraternity brother had been caught in bed with his "little brother" in the fraternity house. Chuck and his grafted siblings were mortified. What this activity meant, they all assumed, was that a man was treating another man like he treated a woman, that some man might treat one of them like a woman. They knew, on some level at least, how distasteful and dehumanizing that often was. Chuck had led the metaphoric lynch mob, jerking pins off the offending chests like motivated migrant farm workers. Chuck considered this portion alone of his fraternal experience to be a part of his training in abnormal psychology, since these were the only queers he'd ever met who weren't incarcerated in one institution or another. The only ones he was aware of anyway. The subject fascinated him and was the only area of psychology that he had rather read about than test and measure. It didn't matter that most of what he read didn't describe his former brothers. He decided that it did, even though he hadn't known either of them well. Then he didn't have to think about them as individuals; he could spend his time taking a position, one that was not exactly missionary: Homosexual men didn't need to be cured; they needed to be locked up somewhere together, which he supposed was a benevolent response to the situation. They would eventually die out and that would be the end of it. Gay women were another matter. Women had tendencies, leanings, wanderings; bent things could be straightened, lost vessels put on course. The fact that he was in a minority in his professional opinion only convinced him that he was right in holding it.

"I've had some experience with homosexuals," he said looking down with as much modesty as he could summon. "There's a certain, well—" He glanced around the room, searching in vain for a hint of the noun he needed. "It's hard to describe without going into a lot of detail. But it fits. And there's probably still time to correct it."

Now her eyes had a curiously sad amusement in them, as if she'd been told a tired joke, one relying heavily on body parts, not wit.

"Really? I didn't realize you'd done so much . . . research in that area, Chuck." The beast was at her lips again. "You don't think your assessment might be a little premature? Tests *have* been mistaken on occasion." Free at last. "One error was actually documented back in '47."

"Elizabeth. This isn't something to joke about," Chuck scolded. "Lisa obviously has a problem. One you're ignoring."

He thought a moment and then smiled and said almost flirtingly, "One that could be dangerous for a woman as attractive as you."

This is getting old, she thought. "In what way?" she said before she could help herself. He seemed flattered.

"It's one thing for a female client to have a healthy transference with a male therapist," he pronounced. "It can get really tricky when it's a same-sex situation. Particularly when there are tendencies involved."

Elizabeth studied him intently. "You're not talking about transference. You're talking about a crush."

"In this case neither would be normal . . . healthy."

"Thank God. At last someone knows what that is."

"What what is?"

"Healthy. The definition's been in so many foster homes."

"Let's not get into the abstract. I'm *trying* to help you." He held up the folder to underline his words. "Evaluation is my field, you know."

"Yes. I know," Elizabeth said as she stood to go. "Counseling is mine." His attempts at superior posturing weren't helping her attitude any. It's been a bad day, she thought, and there's no point in arguing about this with him. "I appreciate your good intentions, your concern for me and for Lisa. But I think I know her better than a test can." She opened the door. "But Lisa's the expert on Lisa. Not a test. Not me. Maybe not even you," she said quietly, her words holding more admonition than her tone.

"You think I'm wrong," he said, sounding almost hurt. "That she's as straight as you or me?"

His phone rang just as she parted her lips, and she took it as a sign from the Almighty that she should seek a neutral corner. This philosophical match could wait.

One more unpleasant item on her list. The last thing she wanted or needed was war with Chuck. But he seemed bent on being right, being the authority on everything. She certainly didn't feel possessive about her clients, and she wanted to believe Chuck was just trying to do his job. Or trying to figure out what it was supposed to be. That would have been difficult enough by itself; it didn't help matters that their esteemed department chairman wasn't diamond clear about what anybody's was supposed to be. Curtis had told Tony and Elizabeth and David that Chuck's responsibilities would be entirely separate from their own and to call on him if they needed him. They didn't need him, so they didn't call, and he wouldn't have had much to do if Curtis hadn't "challenged" Chuck to be "proactive" and find things to help them with. So Chuck went through everything that wasn't locked up offering solutions for solved or non-existent problems. He probably would have done that anyway since that was his nature, but he had even more enthusiasm for butting in if it were officially sanctified in his job description. Chuck's arrogance amid Curtis' confusion only added dust to the desert. Elizabeth needed shade.

Dr. Harrison. Jeanette always offered a little shade.

* * *

PART II

Earlier that year someone in the administration, someone who later would be nearly impossible to indict, decided that the ancient class-change bell system was a noisy, unnecessary nuisance and a waste of money and manhours to maintain. Naturally, a committee was formed. To study the matter. After a semester or so of meetings and minutes and memoranda and surveys of procedures on other campuses, it was more or less concluded that the class-change bells would be disconnected. After all, they were all adults there. Most of whom had watches and could tell time. Some members of the committee expressed doubt on that point but were overruled.

The appointed hour and day for disconnecting the antiquated and complex system approached like the beast toward Bethlehem. The Disconnect Team was informed and prepared.

As informed and prepared as possible.

Some members of the Team were equipped with flat head screwdrivers of every conceivable size; other members carried an equal number with Phillips heads. None thought to carry both. Murphy's Law and all imaginable corollaries, however, made that point moot. The bell housings were attached not by screws but by nuts that were of a unique and indefensible size. The man, who for years had been the only soul to attend to bell maintenance, had months before gone to his semi-final reward by retiring in Key West, saying if it wasn't warm there, he'd just as soon go on to hell.

Only one other man was aware of the insidious little bell nuts and for reasons not known even to himself, he thought bell nuts and their specifications comprised a segment of conventional wisdom. So he remained innocently silent on the matter.

To an independent observer, had there been one, this might not have seemed as difficult as, say, improving world food distribution. But all over campus, underneath scores of unsuspecting bell housings, similar dialogues played out their redundant selves between members of the Sub-teams of the Disconnect Team, who preferred capitalizing on titles to capitalizing on the moment.

"Hell, Homer, the damn thing's too high to reach," said George, looking helplessly up at his rectangular objective, unaware of the hexagonal one yet to come. "You bring a ladder?"

"No," Homer said, slapping his pockets and looking under his feet, searching for the truant ladder. "Guess we'll have to walk all the way back over to the shop. And get one. And carry it all the way back over here. And set it up."

Two hours later and one ladder richer:

"Hell, Homer, the damn thing's held on by a nut. Got a set of nut drivers?"

"No. Got a Phillips head screwdriver, though. Want my Phillips?"

Events and the gods conspired as if to provide examples of indifference and tardiness. And because his men were behind schedule, the Team Supervisor told his Director that everything was moving according to plan.

Plan B, that is. The Team Supervisor then threatened his men with abrupt and irreversible sterility should they continue to fail him. Youth, ambition and a sixteen percent mortgage fueled the impatience of the Team Supervisor. Another stick on the fire was the fact that he was the man who had remained innocently silent about bell nuts.

The campus was notified and prepared for the day toward which the Disconnect Team malaised in a low grade fever, a dangerous new day of independence from bell tyranny.

As notified and prepared as possible.

The chairman of the committee had written the announcement memorandum to the campus community, specifying all pertinent information.

Except the date of disconnect.

His secretary had caught the omission, and knowing that errors made him furious, especially those he himself made, she looked up the date in the last set of minutes and filled in the administrative vacuum.

There had been a typo in the minutes. When the typist had arrived at the part about the date, she had hit a two instead of a three. The Team Supervisor didn't have a copy of the minutes; he had instructions from a meticulous soul who had marked his own calendar at the meeting.

The chairman's secretary typed the memorandum. Twice. The printshop lost the first copy. That is, the secretary said she had sent the first copy. The printshop said they never got the first copy, and there was no work order with the second. Finally printed, too few copies were delivered. To the wrong office.

And then there was Campus Mail. While addressing the reusable envelopes, one secretary found what she suspected was an omen. Inside one of the pouches was an invoice for a copy machine which at that very moment was reiterating happily away somewhere on the other end of the campus. The invoice was marked urgent and past due. It had been touring the campus in search of its innocently delinquent owners for three months.

Even if everything had gone smoother, the bells disconnected on time and the memos out and posted, some members of the committee observed in retrospect that a maximum of thirty-seven people could have been counted on to have actually read of the event. Of those, ten were on the committee, four of whom would have forgotten.

Under the best of circumstances, the regimented, segmented, collective left brain of the campus would have been ill-prepared for a day without audible divisions, where tardiness might prove arbitrary. A day where exits could not be justifiably made in mid-sentence, where long-windedness would not be accompanied by gale warnings.

Dr. Harrison endured one day of the resulting chaos and made a phone call. The class-change bells began ringing again at seven the next day.

* * *

Outside her classroom, Dr. Harrison could hear nine o'clock announcing itself in the hall, as reassuring as a right angle or an edged lawn.

Standing at the podium in front of the class, Dr. Harrison seemed to be studying her notes. She lifted her wirerims away from her face and rubbed the pink footprints they had left on her nose. This class of undergraduates tended to take a few seconds longer to settle, so she would wait, her head down, until absolute silence breathed through the seats. Whether the students thought she was praying or that she had gone to sleep like an old horse, the effect was eventual silence that drifted in like a fog.

Her other colleagues generally thought she was crazy for insisting on teaching a section of undergraduate American history. Able to teach only elite graduate seminars if she chose, why bother with undisciplined children? Required undergraduate courses rarely yielded an abundance of superiority.

But it was the quintessential challenge to Dr. Harrison to take these hundred sets of parched eyes and watch them catch under her flint.

Her requirements a legend on campus, the mentally lazy would avoid her class, if possible. But her name was never listed in the bulletin as the instructor, so avoiding her section had become known as Harrison Roulette. Especially on certain floors of the athletic dorm.

By the second week of class, sometimes sooner, she made sure she knew each student's full name, major and hometown. For the few who might have hoped that the most recent semester break had finally delivered the petitioned senility, a minor demonstration usually dispelled any illusion of relief.

Dr. Harrison cleared her throat in the stillness and swept her eyes slowly across her audience.

"I trust that you scholars avoided autumn's distraction this past weekend." Her eyes paused when they came to Lisa. "Even you, Ms. Hunter." Lisa smiled at the attention. "That you endured not a single blistering forward pass by Mr. Tyler, here."

Sitting next to Lisa, but not as close as he liked, Jake Tyler dropped his eyes in mock modesty and rocked buoy-like from the fraternal jab of a teammate behind him. No one who knew Jake believed that he possessed any modesty, although some objectivity might suggest his looks were more healthy than handsome, his prowess more persistent than innate and his scholarship more C minus than A.

"I'm sure you are all eminently prepared," continued Dr. Harrison, "for today's discussion about the Civil War. More often referred to in the South as simply, 'Thah Waw-wah,' " she said, her last words flowing round and thick like Delta sorghum.

Her voice was more Rhett than Scarlett and tickled the class. Make them smile, she thought, and they might enjoy this in spite of themselves; let the history lie in ambush.

"Let's postpone, for a moment, the tedious. Let's not talk of the dates and the number of dead. Or the parallels or the latitudes. Or the attitudes. Or the beatitudes."

The cadence of her voice had captured them, and they stopped struggling.

"These are the items that make war a thing apparently not worth remembering. I say 'apparently' since men engaged in war so redundantly. Let's talk instead about people. And feelings.

"In order to create the atmosphere necessary for war—or smaller acts of violence—each side must believe that it has the monopoly on such things as people and feelings. It is no easy task to convince an otherwise reasonable man that another human being is not, in fact, another human being. Helpful in this feat of Olympian mental gymnastics is an unpatented device: the stereotype."

Walking around the desk, she leaned against the podium and folded her arms, notes for her lectures having long ago become superfluous.

"Why bother with time-consuming introductions when stereotypes are so convenient. I don't need to know *your* name if I know your group's name, particularly if it's a name I make up myself. If I know you're a Yankee or Johnny Reb, or heaven forefend, a Republican, I am spared the clutter of understanding you. Stereotypes and slaves are very similar in many ways. No one wants to *be* one himself, but *having* them appears to make life so much easier. *Appears* to."

There were no dancing girls in her performance, but her class was as much theatre as academics. For those few who refused to enjoy the show, and there always were a few, she could only feel impatience and a little hurt. Here she was, using everything short of a hat and cane to ease the pain of osmosis, and there sat Jake Tyler, a football playbook not overly hidden inside his notebook.

How consumately unimaginative, she thought. Without a break in voice or stride, she walked to Jake's desk and plucked the intruding diagrams from beneath his nose and returned to her podium, animated and smiling all the while.

Jake's teammate jabbed him again but had the good sense to do it quietly and before Dr. Harrison had turned back around. Languidly, Jake rubbed behind his ear with one finger as if to stifle an itch, but those behind him knew an Italian salute when they saw one.

Jake didn't dislike Dr. Harrison, he just thought she was a ridiculous old woman. How could anybody get excited about *history* for crissake? But *she* did. But then she didn't have anything else to get worked up over. Probably been a thousand years since any man had gotten past Gettysburg with the old biddy. Jake tried to imagine Dr. Harrison as a younger woman, but his attention span was only long enough to reduce her age by a week or so.

He had examined the surface of several thousand topics by the time the bell rang again, none of which had any connection with 1862. But even when the bell rang, and he was supposed to be released, he could always count on his patience, if not his mind, being stretched by at least three more of Dr. Harrison's paragraphs.

Jake couldn't fathom how Lisa could even stay awake in this class, much less be entertained at nine in the morning. He should have gotten Coach to change sections for him. But then there was Lisa and the possibilities that she advertised beneath the name of Calvin Klein. He could stand a little one-hour coma a few times a week for that.

As he and a crowd of others herded toward the door, Dr. Harrison reached over the heads of the passing students, extending Jake's confiscated book toward him. That she was still smiling annoyed Jake; that she had made no comment annoyed him further.

And as usual, Lisa had to stop and say something pleasant to the woman. He always had to wait on her, helping the door jamb support the building.

More aggravating than the professor or the class or the hour of the day was the energy he was expending to get Lisa's undivided attention, which remained a resolutely intact commodity invested elsewhere. In her grades, her intended career, her independence or her virginity. He was firm, though strategically silent in his opinion that for women, those objections were either myth, idle threat or diversionary tactic.

Jake had never had the opportunity to examine these particular opinions of his or any others because he'd never felt close enough or comfortable enough with anyone else to discuss things as threatening as feelings and their consequent conclusions and opinions. He didn't really feel close enough to himself to have more than brief monologues. After these monologues he would feel rather empty and unsatisfied, almost sad; a feeling vaguely like hunger, as if his arms were hungry, aching dully down the insides of them and across his chest. He had this same sensation whenever he knew he was lonely, a condition he avoided by whatever means possible.

He felt the ache often with Lisa when he wanted to talk to her but was afraid she'd laugh when he had neither engineered her laughter nor been in the mood to appreciate it. But now, in the crowded hall outside Dr. Harrison's class, he wasn't feeling anything but the need to touch Lisa. She always seemed like a space traveler after this class, not in the same time zone, thinking about everything but who she was with.

Finally in the hall with Lisa, he was able to get her eyes, if not her mind or hands, on him. For no more than four paces. Then she was gone. Snatched from him in the instant his eyes were diverted by another pair of tight jeans. He was addled for an instant as he wheeled, searching for her in mid-sentence, his infinitive split. It was as if the Rapture had come.

Lisa felt her balance suddenly misplaced in a disconcerting softness and then strong hands on her shoulders correcting the mid-hall collision. She had her feet to find, then her breath, then the face belonging to the hands. A sphincter muscle somewhere near her middle contracted in recognition, the soft friction lighting a fuse that ran to her lips, exploding her face in a smile.

"Dr. McKay!" Lisa exhaled. "Hi!" Lisa stepped back, suddenly embarrassed. "Sorry . . . should have been watching where I was going. You're not hurt, are you?"

"Uh-uh," said Elizabeth, smiling like a conspirator, remembering the phrase from their last meeting. "I'm not fragile either, Lisa."

Her embarrassment chased by Elizabeth's smile, Lisa's eyes crinkled in answer, her expression decidedly more entertained than the one cast at Jake, who appeared at her elbow like an afterthought.

"Oh, Dr. McKay, this is Jake. Jake Tyler." Jake had slid his hand around Lisa's waist, possession in the crook of his elbow, a hint of jealousy in his eyes that Lisa's smile had not been at his bidding. Neither his ego nor his id would have called it jealousy; they would both have called it lack of sleep. "Jake, Dr. McKay."

McKay. He recognized the name, having heard it a million times from Lisa. When she wasn't in class, she was seeing this shrink. Didn't even care if people knew. Said it was no different than talking to a professor about a grade.

He said he wouldn't be caught dead with a shrink. Seeing Elizabeth, he thought maybe naked was how he'd prefer being caught with this one. Then he remembered he was pissed. Somehow Dr. McKay was connected in his mind with several thwarted attempts to be with Lisa. Appointments or ideas stemming from appointments or God knows what; and since it couldn't be Jake's lack of charisma, it had to be something, so why not this feminist? He wasn't sure what one was, but he thought she was one, and he didn't need to know anything else.

"So, you're the lady taking up so much of Lisa's time." Jake's lips curled up looking for all the world like a smile, but his voice hit the dew point of rudeness.

Had he been ready or inclined to read more body language than a head fake, he would have seen a paragraph in Elizabeth's glance. She continued to smile at Lisa, half winked, shaking Lisa loose from the hook of Jake's sarcasm, then smiled at Jake.

"I hear you're the only hope for a decent season, Jake," Elizabeth said, meaning it and the smile. She glanced at her watch. "Have to run. Got to catch somebody. Jake, nice to meet you. Have a good game on Saturday. You take care, Lisa."

Jake was only temporarily confused, then accepted the flattery as his due until he saw Lisa's admiring eyes following Elizabeth's retreating back down the hall. Feeling his eyes on her, Lisa's narrowed and turned accusingly on him.

"What's with you?" she flared. "Why were you so rude to her?"

"What do you care?" he said, his voice cockily teasing. "You queer for that shrink or something?"

Pinching the air between their eyes in a withering stare, Lisa set her jaw to snap a ten-penny nail and clamped it for a full silent sentence until she was sure he had heard the clang, then turned in the emptying corridor, not caring if he followed but certain he would. He made her so goddamn mad with his smartass comments sometimes that she could spit. Other times he made her laugh. He never knew which it was going to be. Neither did she. Or why, despite her attempts to find a reason for nearly everything. But she knew exactly why she put up with his arrogance, even liked him. He was taller than she was, which was rare; he was a celebrity which meant she was envied and noticed by women even prettier than she was; and he was intensely frivolous, which made her not think so much. She analyzed everything to exhaustion, and he was a respite. Besides, no one had ever paid this kind of attention to her, no one had ever courted her so feverishly. She couldn't discover an adequate reason why she wasn't asked out as often as other girls, except perhaps that she was too tall and didn't have a talent for flirting. She also never let a boy beat her at anything that she could do better. Her father had warned her that winning was not a wise strategy for women, given that winnings and strategies were male things. Things like givens made some people accept any conclusion. Lisa wanted to think that she questioned even the givens. She was questioning givens today, and Jake's lack of seriousness and his possessiveness were wearing on her nerves.

Jake watched Lisa stride down the hall away from him, and he rolled his eyes and notified the gods of his bewilderment. Their response being benign neglect, he looked to Lisa's unfulfilled possibilities as they carried her down the hall. Finally he surrendered to the dependable rule of the despot gonad, shrugged and loped down the hall to her side.

Silence. Around a ten-penny jaw. A clown, he jumped in front of her, dancing backward down the hall, all dazzling, contrite apologies in pantomime. Then dejected surrender.

"I was just joking, Lisa. Jeez. You take everything so serious."

"I'd do better to make everything a joke like you?" she said, biting the tips of her words angrily. "Great. Then we could both flunk out."

"It's only a couple of courses," Jake said defensively. "If it weren't for that Harrison bitch. Coach even asked her to lighten up. Said Harrison practically threw him out of her office."

"You might try studying once in a while," Lisa said, adding a pinch of causticity to flavor the meat of her anger. "We're lucky to even have Dr. Harrison. She could teach at any school she wanted. And this is the only undergraduate course she offers."

Rubbing his nose, he assumed the professor's voice and inflection. "She's lucky I condescend to attend her class," he imitated.

His performance obviously entertained Jake, but he was an audience of one. Lisa clung to her anger like tendrils of ivy.

Well, hell, Jake thought, if humility is the only way . . .

"Look, Lisa," Jake said as seriously as he could manage, "I'm sorry about how I acted to Dr. McKay. It just seems like you're always over there. What do you need her for, anyway? You should talk to *me* if something's bothering you."

Some days you eat the bear, some days the bear eats you. Lisa had been searching all day for that elusive semi-final straw, and now she'd spotted it. She looked at him frostily. He knew it was third and long.

"We've been over this a thousand times, Jake. She's helping me sort some things out. That's *all*. You don't own me. If that's what you want, find someone who *wants* to be a lackey."

She turned on her heel and walked away. Why am I putting myself through this, he thought. But of course, that was a rhetorical question.

At the end of the hall there sat a row of nondescript people who belonged to some organization dedicated to community service, charity, scholarship and beer kegs. They were at that moment being bored to distraction selling flowers to raise money for something or other. Jake burrowed in his pocket, pulled out some money and snatched a bouquet without waiting for his change. Thundering out the door, he caught up with Lisa on the sidewalk.

God alone knew what hormones thrashed around in Lisa's veins. Jake was certainly without a clue, because he saw her smile as she took the flowers, as if she'd never been upset at all. Bewildered but relieved, he thought he'd avoid saying anything controversial. What's a safe subject, he thought. Zoysia grass? Photosynthesis? Quarks? Remembering virtually nothing about the areas of horticulture, botany or nuclear physics, he lit on gossip.

"You heard from Nita since she got married?"

Lisa's face immediately fell. Jake couldn't fathom exactly what emotion he detected in her voice, but he suspected somehow he'd stepped in something. Again.

"No." Her voice almost broke when she said it.

Jake looked at her. "Not at all? It's been months. I talk to Bobby all the time. What a waste. He's acting like a husband already. Anyway, I thought Nita was supposed to be your best friend."

Hurt and anger. He saw it then, but he was even more confused than before. "Yeah," she said, "supposed to be. Could we just not talk about her? She's *not* my best friend. Not anymore."

Guess I'll have to read up on quarks, he thought. Nothing's safe anymore.

*   *   *

Maybe other people can carry briefcases, thought Dr. Harrison, but there's certainly nothing succinct about mine. She stood at her desk trying to fit her papers and books back into her aging satchel.

Rituals made life appear under control, and she had a thousand of them. The contents of her satchel, the day on which she polished it, the spot in which she parked her pen never varied. The stacks of books and papers in her office at first gave the impression of clutter, from the sheer magnitude of it. But as she said frequently, clutter is as clutter does. It's only clutter if you don't know where anything is or why it's there.

She looked up over her glasses as she massaged her nose and saw Elizabeth standing in the doorway.

"And what brings you to these callowed halls?" Dr. Harrison smiled as she moved toward Elizabeth, whose mouth was a soft, full curve that didn't completely mask the tension in her eyes. Dr. Harrison peered over her glasses at Elizabeth's bad mood.

"Someone's killed your pet rock." She assumed the position of a police inspector with an imaginary note pad and pencil. "Who?" she said, poising the nonexistent lead as a prologue to extinction. "It was his or her last official act."

No way to stay in a bad mood around this woman, Elizabeth thought, and she pursed her lips and looked off toward her imagination, as if trying to think of a riddle to pose.

"Who," mused Elizabeth, "in our acquaintance have we always suspected of receiving his doctorate from the Post Office?"

"I assume the pronoun is indicative, not generic?"

Elizabeth nodded once, slowly. Her eyes twinkled.

"Your clues aren't much help. We know at least . . . oh, say, twenty-nine." She knew exactly who the culprit was, who it had been for a year, when Elizabeth came to her in the middle of the day with that look in her eyes.

"A hint then," Elizabeth sighed. "He has two heads. Faces, anyway."

"Oh, but it isn't possible. You don't mean—?"

They were both smiling now at their game and enunciated the name slowly in an often rehearsed duet.

"Little Freddie Curtis," they sang.

Dr. Harrison shook her head in true exasperation. "Well, we knew that with his history, it was only a matter of time. What's he done this trip?"

* * *

They walked across campus and found a corner seat in the faculty dining room while Elizabeth explained the situation about Fred and her salary. Dr. Harrison sat silently listening.

Elizabeth picked up her coffee cup, discovering for the fourth time that it was still empty, and looked at Dr. Harrison across the table from her. At this time of the morning, hardly anyone else was in the faculty cafeteria, and her cup hitting its saucer sounded like the metal ball inside a steeple bell.

"Four thousand dollars isn't even subtle," Dr. Harrison said, making little rocking motions with her head in disbelief. "But then, subtlety implies a degree of intelligence. In Fred, that possibility has long since been eliminated."

"I told you there'd be problems when they created that position for him." Elizabeth was disgusted. "When a *woman* makes too many mistakes, she's fired. An inept man just gets responsibility for smaller and smaller budgets."

"Maybe they thought you psychologists could bring out his hidden potential."

"As a human being, maybe. As an administrator, no."

Dr. Harrison looked intently at Elizabeth. "You don't need my counsel on this."

Elizabeth was already tired, and it had hardly begun. "I know what I have to do. I just wanted you to know what I've already done."

A flash of mischief curled around Dr. Harrison's eyes and pushed at the corners of her mouth. "Sue him, Elizabeth. It'd be good for their collective liver."

"May I remind you, madame, that you are the one who's always telling me to 'use the system to change the system.' " Elizabeth put quotation marks in the air with her fingers and dropped her voice into a replica of Dr. Harrison's.

"Don't quote me to me. That angers sage and wizened old people. It's embarrassing when we have the need to contradict ourselves."

Smiling ruefully, Elizabeth studied her coffee cup and wiped the crescent of her lipstick from the rim. "It's just too obvious. Even to Fred. He *must* know he has to correct this. It's the law."

"Believe me, Elizabeth. He has a variety of options besides those of seeing reason or being fair. Much less admitting a mistake."

"I have to believe that people are capable of good intentions, Jeanette. Even Fred."

Her eyebrows rising with a tide of doubt, Dr. Harrison shook her head. "Your world view may be somewhat nearsighted in Fred's case. His heart and his vocabulary have always had the same problem: They both may be big enough, but they are *forever* in the wrong place."

This was their other practiced duet: Dr. Harrison's laughter rumbled around in baritone; Elizabeth's lilted into alto.

"Like when I was the '*blunt* of the *issue*'?" Elizabeth laughed and her face and voice slid down into an impression of Fred's more serious attempts. " 'You need to be more enthusiastic about this, Lizbuth. More *exhorbitant*.' " Rolling her eyes toward Dr. Harrison, she switched channels to her own voice and spoke as if correcting Fred, patiently, as if to a first grader. "Ex-u-ber-ant, Fred. Exuberant." She launched her eyes heavenward and raised both palms in divine beseechment. "*Help* me."

"I could, you know," Dr. Harrison announced seriously. "Thirty years ago, the president of this university learned the value of mental discipline as a student of mine . . . when he found himself forced to take American history for a *second* time."

Everyone knew of the friendship that had grown between the professor and her former student who now led the school. She had even been instrumental in getting Geoff Meade to return to the University two years ago, waging a masterful campaign for his appointment. President Geoffrey Meade now called on Dr. Harrison as his official and unofficial advisor in nearly everything on which he needed the inside skinny or the detailed history. Or when he needed someone to analyze the factions and negotiate precisely the correct solution. For her part, she couldn't remember a more astute mind in any of her classes, once she had gotten his attention. She felt like a proud parent and a respected friend to him, a combination difficult to house in the same relationship. It had to do with one's sense of respect and honor, and while he hadn't learned his code from Dr. Harrison, he had certainly refined it because of her, and he said so often and publicly.

Dr. Harrison looked intently at Elizabeth, "Boys aren't the only ones who can play Good Ole Boy, Elizabeth."

Elizabeth shook her head quickly. "No, Jeanette. I know how much you hate playing that game. I asked Fred for an answer by Monday. It's got nothing to do with can or can't. People do what they *want* to do. And the Lord may yet smile on me. I've only asked for justice."

Dr. Harrison's hand flew to her heart, and she clutched at her blouse in pretended horror. "Oh, no, Elizabeth! Never ask for justice. Ask for mercy! Mercy!"

* * *

"Mercy, Fred. How do you engineer these God awful disasters? Do you sit up nights *planning* how to ruin my day?"

Curtis looked sheepishly at Sam Fitzhugh as they sat in Sam's office among all his souvenirs of legal battles won and lost. On Sam's desk the scales of Blind Justice held loose change so that Sam wouldn't clank when he walked. Sam thought jingling pockets were an indication of little, if any, breeding.

"Come on Sam. It's not that bad." Curtis maintained a forced smile. "Is it?"

Fitzhugh looked at Curtis with a mixture of impatience and pity, his look his only response. Curtis shifted in his seat and reached in his pants pocket to fidget noisily with what was left of his lunch money, then looked helplessly at Fitzhugh, and his forced smile seceded from his lips. As usual, Curtis couldn't understand what the problem was. Somehow, Sam said that something was wrong and that Curtis had caused it. Curtis had done as he was told, and somehow it was wrong anyway. He always felt like he had come late to the huddle, missed the play being called and couldn't hear the signals at the line. Sometimes he wasn't even sure he had on the right uniform or knew the name of the game.

"What could I *do*, Sam? Staff psychologists aren't bought cheap, ya know?"

"Is a *class action suit* cheap, Fred?"

"Does it come with a vest?" Curtis' smile climbed back on his face, surveyed an unappreciative audience, lost its grip and slid slowly into the cleft of his chin.

"Fred, sometimes I don't understand you. What on earth possessed you to pull this stunt?"

"*I* didn't set those salaries." Fred was getting defensive now. "I've only been in that job a year. *I* can't help it if their salaries were too low to start with."

"You could have *asked* somebody, Fred, before making Chuck's salary final." He sighed tiredly, closed his eyes, then looked back at Curtis. "How'd you get approval to hire a new man, anyway?" Have to give the man some kind of credit, Sam thought. Fred must have gotten his degree in finagling.

"That part was easy," Curtis said with chagrin. "You know Chuck's old man. Practically owns the Athletic Department. Played college ball with Dr. Thompson. So Thompson calls *me*." A pleading look came into his eyes. "Jesus, Sam. Thompson's my boss, for crissake. Says he, 'See what you can find for Gardner's boy.' What was I supposed to *do*?"

A ripple of understanding washed across Fitzhugh's face. "But, Fred . . . four thousand more than the rest of your staff? You can do a favor without breaking the law. Not to mention Personnel policy, even if it is new. We're already under the Federal gun about our salary situation."

What frustrated Fitzhugh was that he never knew for sure whether the gun was loaded. But every four years or so, the boys in Washington would start making equal rights noises for the benefit of the ladies in the audience and make a big show of cracking down on some major institution so they'd get their pictures in the paper. There'd be committees and studies and reports and allegations and law suits, and when the dust settled not much would have changed except the money in some lawyer's pocket. His included. He loved this business. People like Curtis were making him rich.

"Jesus, Sam." Curtis sat rubbing his worried face. "I thought the salary was within range. I thought . . . shit, I . . . I didn't *think* . . . that is, well. . . ." Curtis continued his exhibition of not thinking and finally stopped when a thought managed to strike him a glancing blow. "Hell, I didn't think Chuck would be stupid enough to go around announcing it to everybody."

The fact that Martha Huddleston also knew because she had processed all the paper work and did all of the bookkeeping didn't occur to him. It also didn't occur to him that if Martha didn't tell her, all Elizabeth had to do was look it up in the state capital library since state tax expenditures were by law a matter of public record. This particular public law was one that men in his position pretended didn't exist. They had told employees that salaries were confidential for so long that they had begun to believe it themselves, thus performing the alchemy of changing myth into fact. Curtis knew that the state salaries weren't supposed to be secret, but the state to him was the governor and the senators and the highway patrol, all of whom he felt were overpaid. *His* tax supported budget and *their* tax supported budget had nothing to do with each other as far as he was concerned. He ought to be able to digest his slice of the pie anyway he wanted, and it was Chuck and his fat mouth that had made Curtis look like he had meringue on his face.

Curtis was truly angry now that he had located whom to blame for his predicament. "If he'd kept his damn mouth shut—"

"But he didn't. Now you've got to ask Thompson for . . . looks like about fifteen thousand to get everybody in line."

Ask *Thompson*? Curtis thought, horrified. Why don't you just tell me to board the train to Auschwitz?

"Jesus God, Sam! I'd rather roller skate in a snake pit then be in the same room with Thompson! He doesn't even *like* me." His eyes wandered off in search of escape and found Fitzhugh's golf putter resting against a bookcase. He brightened slightly. "You play golf with him, Sam. Couldn't you—"

Fitzhugh's hand shot up as if he had been seized with the spirit. "Not *that* often, I don't." He paused and looked at Curtis, knowing precisely where Curtis was coming from, though not the foggiest about how he got there. "Look, I'm not a bit happier about this affirmative action shit than you are."

Fitzhugh stood and walked to his door, silently announcing the beginning of his closing argument. "If you didn't have Elizabeth on your staff, you could probably invent some excuse for paying Gardner more than the other men." One hand rested on the door knob, the other in the air of resignation. "As it is . . . well, Fred, I've got enough to do without another class action suit cluttering my day." He opened the door. "I don't care how you do it, Fred. But I'll tell you one thing. You'd better not let her get to court. 'Cause if you do, you'll lose. It would cause a very expensive chain reaction. And *believe* me, Fred. *This* time the powers that be would not be lenient on the man who lit the fuse."

The already pained expression on Curtis' face became a stricken one. Curtis walked tiredly out of Fitzhugh's office and down the hall. His head felt fuzzy and he couldn't think, although that wasn't what he wanted to do anyway. He wanted to push the hold button in his head. He needed a vacation or a sabbatical, although he didn't know what either of those were really, since he preferred being at work to going on trips with his wife, and he certainly preferred the office to the library.

It was already after five, but he didn't want to go home. He needed to get his brain clear, needed to be alone, so he headed for the men's room. There were few places left in the world where a man could pull himself together, and he was thankful the ERA hadn't passed for he believed he would have lost even this porcelain sanctuary. Of course, the sanctuary itself provided its own set of tensions because there was always the urinal with its intrinsic probability of public exposure and negative comparisons with the other friars. Too short, too strange, too thin, too something. The possibilities for inferiority were endless.

Fortunately he was alone. After relieving himself, he splashed cold water on his face and the back of his neck until his head felt better. With relief he remembered that tonight was his wife's real estate class, and she wouldn't be home until he could appear to be involved in something else. There was always a game on cable that he could watch so he wouldn't have to think or respond to his wife. Football had almost the same soothing effect on him that bourbon had and with no headache unless you actually played the game.

He walked to his car, threaded his way across campus and inched into the speeding traffic. Other cars had to downshift and pull exasperatedly around him, since he never seemed to be aware of his speed relative to anyone else's. He saw a drugstore and wondered if they were out of Vanquish at home, but as soon as he flipped on his left blinker he forgot what he was turning for, and eventually forgot even that he had intended to turn, but the blinker stayed on. All the way home, even when he made the last of several unannounced right turns into his driveway, hundreds of strangers were forced to be needlessly cautious, expecting him to turn left just because he was flashing that he would. His signal clucked, blinked, urged, reminded, nagged, but his radio was shouting about downs and yardage and formations. And he wasn't even listening to that.

* * *

"You wanted to see me, Fred?" Chuck poked his head in Curtis' open office door. The cable football had done no good. It was 8 o'clock in the morning and Curtis had had little sleep the night before.

Looking out the window, Curtis stood watching the swelling ranks of would-be runners who hiked round and round the track outside his office. Curtis didn't understand the attraction that going in circles held for these people. He looked from the window irritably over his shoulder at Chuck and motioned for him to sit down. In his hand Curtis slowly turned a plastic cube displaying pictures of his somewhat hefty wife and two collegiate sons.

He rarely looked at the pictures, but he played with the cube all the time. It was a puzzle easier to work than the Rubik's cube on the coffee table, because the picture cube seemed to have no moving parts. But he had yet to master either.

Curtis walked across the room to the door as Chuck sank relaxed into the couch. When Curtis closed the door, Chuck knew something was up and sat at attention, carefully watching the man in front of him, noting the tension in his jaw, and the fact that Curtis was looking everywhere but at him.

Sitting across from Chuck, Curtis aborted the pregnant pause by thwacking his picture cube down on the table. He traded in one unsolved riddle for another and began fooling with Rubik's.

"How's your father, Chuck?" Curtis didn't sound overly concerned with the man's condition. Chuck knew this wasn't the topic sentence.

"Fine."

"He pleased that you're working at his Alma Mater?"

"Very much."

Turning and turning the pieces of the cube, Curtis watched his unsuccessful hands as a frown plowed across his forehead. He sucked in half the air in the room and let it out in a belabored sigh before he spoke, his tone sharper than before.

"If you intend to keep this job, Chuck, there are some things you'd best learn about how to play on my team. One of them is knowing when to keep your mouth shut."

Puzzled and defensive, Chuck tried to figure out what game he was supposed to be playing. Curtis was warming to his subject, enjoying the flawless, polished surface of righteous indignation.

"I *told* you in the beginning that salary information is confidential. Damn straight, I did. Damn straight."

Chuck dropped his jaw to claim ignorance of this new information, but Curtis was squirting too much adrenalin to slow down for a conversation.

"If you hadn't told Lizbuth, she'd never have found out what you're making."

"But, Fred—" Chuck attempted.

The older man sliced off the end of the sentence, this time distressing the table top with the toy in his hand. He stood and sauntered to the window, his back to Chuck.

"I really hate that your first month has started like this, Chuck. Because of you, Lizbuth is threatening to sue the University," he continued resentfully. "*Gave* me 'til Monday to raise her salary." He turned toward Chuck and slung another wad of mud. "Legal office isn't happy about what you caused either. Damned affirmative action! A man can't make his own decisions anymore."

Now Chuck knew the name of the game: Let's You and Him Fight.

"If she were doing her damn job, she wouldn't have time to be nosing around in your business," Chuck offered.

"She does *her* job, Chuck," Curtis threatened.

Something licked sharply at the inside of Chuck's stomach, a little drop of adrenalin, a little fear. He watched Curtis carefully and began to calculate his position. His hands sought something to do, found Curtis' Polish cube and began unconsciously clicking the squares expertly into position.

"You're really the blunt of this whole issue, Chuck. The *blunt*." Curtis shook his head almost sadly now, his tone softening from anger to scolding, then to disappointment. "I'm sure your father wanted you to do well here. So did I. . . ."

Chuck's jaw tightened at the pointed mention of his father, with whom he had had another shouting match only the night before. Nothing he did pleased that man, and it infuriated Chuck that his father could still make him feel like a little boy, hurt and vulnerable.

Curtis turned from the window, and seeing that Chuck was about to launch into a defense in earnest, he abruptly held up his palm to stop him.

Then he poured himself into his swivel chair, which was still badly in need of tuning, and he squeaked back to prop his feet on his desk. His aim had never been extraordinary, and he had a hard time finding the empty space between the phone and his cup of worn-out ink pens. He hit the receiver and it rattled around on the desk, escaped his lunge and fell to the floor. A grin threatened to rampage across Chuck's face, and Chuck had to corral it with his hand.

Curtis' rosy, embarrassed face softened a little, and he dropped his voice a notch in the hierarchy to that of a forgiving father as he replaced the receiver.

"I know you didn't mean any harm. You're new. It takes a while to learn the system, Chuck. I've had some tough cases in my time," he added with more than a hint of self-importance. "Always kept the upper handle. People *used* to know how to act around the man in charge. Damn straight, they did."

Chuck continued to click the little colored squares, the puzzle almost complete, his eyes still calculating his position with Curtis. "Don't you have any, well, leverage with her, Fred? She doesn't *owe* you for anything?"

Now I'm getting through, Curtis thought, and smiled like a losing coach who's just found a new quarterback. "You mean, do I have any dirt on her. No. No dirt. She does nasty things like return borrowed ink pens. And she never borrows them from me."

"Come *on*, Fred. Nobody's that good. She's got to have a chink."

Curtis snorted, looking almost disappointed. "Chink? She doesn't even use the word to describe those slanty-eyed little bastards. If she's got a chink, I wish I knew about it," he said.

"She's got one, Fred. Believe me."

* * *

"How about a drink for the shrinks?" Chuck hung from the side of the doorframe like a gymnast and smiled his All-American smile.

Elizabeth looked tiredly over her stack of work at him and then at her watch and rubbed the bridge of her nose.

"Just a quickie?" he said.

She hesitated, then nodded. "Let me make a call first."

As she dialed the number and waited, she gathered the folders in front of her and locked them in her desk. Chuck prowled her office, absorbing what he thought was an accurate picture of the woman who had furnished it. A photograph caught his eyes, and he picked it up to look at the woman next to Elizabeth. Woof, he thought, look at this hot little piece hanging on Elizabeth. Even more my type than the good doctor here. He wondered if this was the "Kincaid" she and Tony kept referring to. Maybe he could wrangle an introduction from Tony. He set the picture down and picked up one that showed Tony with his arms around Elizabeth. He sure is a handsome devil, thought Chuck. He turned and hastily considered his own reflection in the window pane. He had good taste and knew a handsome man when he saw one, but he would certainly never have voiced any complementary comments about another man's looks. He had been raised to say that men were ugly, no matter how good looking they were.

"Hey, Favorite," Elizabeth said softly into the phone. "No, I'll be home in about an hour." She closed her eyes and smiled secretively at whatever was being suggested to her by the disembodied voice in her ear. "Please," she laughed, "this is a *business* phone . . . . I know you do . . . . Me, too, Angel."

Chuck watched her face and listened to her purring voice. That lucky bastard, he thought, but maybe Tony needs a little competition to keep him on his toes. He thought of all the men as opponents when it came to women, but from what he could see of Tony, he considered him to be worthy adversary: rugged and masculine, a former Marine Corps officer, Ivy League diplomas. But he sure was touchy and possessive about his work. Chuck had tried to help him several times and gotten a dirty look for his trouble. But his relationship with Tony didn't much bother Chuck; what he was concentrating on now was getting inside Elizabeth's head, and if he were as successful as usual, into somewhere else as well. Either or both of those activities could be scheduled earlier when helped along with a little Chivas. And there was a bar not a hundred yards away.

The bar across the street from the University was almost an unofficial branch campus; graduate students and young professors continued their seminars while they adjusted their attitudes and oiled their imaginations. Chuck led Elizabeth to a corner table and sucked down one Scotch and half of another before Elizabeth could sip half a glass of Chablis.

"I don't know that it would be fair to say my father is domineering," said Chuck, poking at the ice in his glass with one finger. "He didn't cut me out of the will *completely* when I dropped out of law school. My Ph.D. redeemed me. And taking this job at his old school has straightened my halo even further." He took a long swig of his drink and eyed Elizabeth penetratingly over the rim of his glass. "So, what about you? A good-looking woman like you ought to be married, making good-looking babies."

Wear me *out*, she thought. But she smiled lightly. "Was it part of your graduate work, or were you born with this compulsion for clichés?"

Chuck leaned away from her, studying her across the roadblocks she kept erecting in the air between them. Not many women in his history had been able or inclined to remain ambulatory under the weight of his brand of masculine charm. Elizabeth's neutrality hadn't gotten to the point of hurting his feelings yet; so he was still responding to her lack of enthusiasm as a challenge.

"Just don't like to waste time is all," he said, still determined. "You engaged to Tony or something?"

"Or something."

"Next time I'll get his permission to take you out."

She was still smiling, but she hoped he would hear her in spite of her remaining light about it. "That might be a little redundant. Can't you understand the word *no* unless you hear it from another man?"

"I haven't heard it from anybody yet."

"That's a little difficult to believe."

"You came out with me, didn't you?"

She gave a little laugh as if remembering a private, inside joke. "Not . . . really. This isn't a date."

Not one to abandon an attractive pursuit, his eyes wandered over her face and body. Staring usually made reluctant conquests nervous: the silence, the implied touching, the power of scrutiny. Elizabeth just sat there like a bump on a pickle. What was the key to this woman?

"There's nothing more frustrating to a man than a woman who's or-somethinged," he sighed.

She shrugged. "Undoubtedly, Chuck, there are millions of women whose sole purpose on the face of the earth is specifically to frustrate you. But then, frustration is the result of the view that you are the only person with the right to say 'no.' "

He considered that for a moment and for some reason thought of his father.

"Well, anyway, I had another reason for wanting to get you alone. Talk to you that is." He took the last gulp of his drink and hailed the waiter for another. "I hear I'm caught in the middle of your salary problem. Maybe it would help if I talked to Fred for you."

"Thank you, but I don't need an interpreter. I speak bureaucratese." She looked down at her wine and then back at him. "Look, Chuck, you're not in the middle as far as I'm concerned. I don't blame you. You're caught in the system like the rest of us: Pay as little as you can get by with, and keep it secret so you *can* pay as little as you can get by with."

"If you're part of an organization, Elizabeth, you either play by its rules or you get out."

She snorted at that. "The problem is that the published rules are selectively applied. Besides, I'm not playing. If I were, I certainly wouldn't spell the game W.A.S.P.M."

He thought for a moment. White Anglo Saxon Protestant Male. Him.

"Whoa! Jump back, Jack. I didn't know feminists wore dresses."

"I'm not into power games, Chuck. Not even feminist ones. And you?" Her voice was getting an edge to it. "I wouldn't want to misjudge your character."

"That's a dangerous thing for a psychologist to do."

She looked steadily at him and said pointedly, "Yes. It is." She looked at her watch. "Look, I've got to go."

"Come on. It's early yet." But then, seeing her resolve, he shrugged and pushed his chair back as she stood. "I'll walk you to your car."

"That's ok. You stay. There's an English prof over there all alone. Pretty one, too."

"No, I insist," he said with an exaggerated bow toward the door. She flipped up her hands, tossed a ten on the table and headed for the door. The waiter arrived with his drink and Chuck downed it in long gulps.

Ok, Miss Feminist, he thought. Pay for the drinks, open your own door. I can play this any way you want it.

Outside, he went directly to his car, got in and watched while she was still finding her key. He still couldn't get over the rush he got at seeing the shape of her through that gauzy stuff she always wore.

"Wait, Elizabeth," he shouted. "I just remembered something." He reached behind the seat and gathered a load of books. Climbing unsteadily out of the car he handed her the stack.

"What's this?" she said, leaning against her little silver sports car.

"Well, after our discussion about Lisa Hunter, I dug these out at home. You might skim through them before we review her again."

She examined the titles and sighed. He's just trying to be helpful, she told herself. Yes, she answered, but it would improve things if he'd stop acting as if he were The Source. Or The Force.

"Even if these were pertinent, I'm afraid they wouldn't be helpful. I've read them. They deal only with Gay men. But what's a mother to do? Men are the subjects of most books, aren't they? But if it would be helpful to you, I'll look at them again and we can talk."

He leaned against her car and looked into her eyes. The Scotch was taking hold of his libido, and his resolve to take a new tack with her sailed away on the wind.

"Can't you honestly think of anything more helpful to me than talk?" he said huskily.

She stopped him with a chilly look. "I doubt it." She opened the car door between them, and he rested his bruised ego against her hood.

"Let's get one thing clear," she said, none too gently. "Lisa is my client. If she prefers to see you instead, that's fine. Until then, hang your scarlet letters on somebody else."

"My, my," he said down his nose, "aren't we getting defensive? If I didn't know better, I'd almost say you had a personal interest in the subject."

"We've discussed a few. Which one? Sixteenth century chauvinism or early American literature? Or middle American psychology?"

She got in and closed the door. "I don't really think we need to continue this discussion, Chuck. I don't think there's much chance either of us will have a change of heart. Or of mind." Then as an afterthought, "You be careful driving home."

* * *

Students were killing time all around her. Martha, however, was resuscitating as much of it as she could get her hands on. Her fingers whizzed atop her typewriter, and she caught the phone on the first bounce; she continued to type while she spoke.

"Good morning," she crooned, "Counseling Services . . . . Oh, hey, Kincaid. Listen. I need legal advise from my favorite lawyer. Can I get Workman's Comp for chronic boney fingers? These people are working me slap to *death*." She laughed as she listened. "Ok. No, she didn't schedule appointments today. Some report or other. Just a sec." She punched the hold button, then the intercom. "Elizabeth? It's Kincaid."

She plopped the phone back in its cradle and swooped back to her typing.

Chuck came trooping down the hall and halted her at her desk. "Got that report ready yet, Martha?"

She looked up slowly but continued to type. "No, Dr. Gardner. I don't. I can't read your writing," she said as pleasantly as she could muster. "I can do a lot of complex things, but not that."

He didn't appreciate her attitude but slowly blinked his temper under control. "Then let me help you, Martha." The sarcasm was barely masked. He reached over her shoulder and opened the folder containing his material sitting next to her typewriter. "This, Martha, is an *A* and this is a *B*," he said condescendingly, "and so on throughout what is commonly known as the alphabet."

"Which one?" she said, now mildly sarcastic herself. "Sanskrit?"

Before he could take a breath, Elizabeth whipped out of her office as if she'd been fitted with roller skates. She threw her words over her shoulder at Martha as she charged out of the office door.

"It's my cat, Martha! A dogfight! She's at the vet's! Lock my office for me!"

As Elizabeth vanished, Chuck glared at Martha and slowly picked up his handwritten sheets, stacking them inside his folder. "Never mind, Martha. Elizabeth needs to read this anyway before it goes out. If she can read it, surely you can manage."

Fred's going to hear about this shit. He's been easy on that woman too long, he thought as he walked into Elizabeth's office. Who the hell does Martha think she is? Probably didn't get beyond high school. Bitch.

He picked up one of Elizabeth's pens, scratched a note to her and clipped the sheet to the folder. He looked around the office as he unconsciously put the pen in his shirt pocket and catalogued the contents of her desk. Stacks of folders were piled next to her appointment calendar, and as he set his own among them and turned to go, something he saw on her desk registered and pulled his head back round.

On the tab of the folder next to his, written in Elizabeth's precisely flowing hand, was a name.

Lisa Hunter.

* * *

45

PART III

"Angel, precious. Who's my favorite?"

Elizabeth's voice almost sang in a soft contralto. Lying on her bed with Elizabeth about a foot away was a stunning woman who looked as though she'd just left a modeling assignment, perhaps high fashion, perhaps Soloflex. The woman's long, tight body almost matched Elizabeth's but was more athletic, harder, with the grace of a runner, while Elizabeth's flowed as if in a ballet.

Elizabeth's eyes were not on the woman, but somewhere on the bed between them, and her hand moved toward the spot. There on the bed lay an enormous cat, with even more enormous ears, little bandages on her feet and cat consternation on her face. But she was purring in spite of herself.

"Elizabeth," Kincaid said soothingly, almost purring like the cat, "she'll be fine. She just wore her toenails off a little while moving a tad too hastily down the driveway. Believe me, the fight wasn't nearly as damaging as the retreat." Kincaid touched the cat and then Elizabeth's face. "She's been plotting revenge on that dog. I can tell."

Elizabeth's eyes misted, and a tear of relief and foolishness escaped over the rim before she could catch it. It ran down to Kincaid's waiting finger, and she lifted it off Elizabeth's cheek and wiped it on the cat's head. The cat shot Kincaid a dirty look.

"I know you think this is silly, Kincaid," Elizabeth said, wiping her eyes and allowing an embarrassed laugh, "but I *love* this kitty. You didn't grow up with animals as your best friends."

Rolling back on her elbows, Kincaid smiled mischievously, her eyebrows bouncing as she knocked the ashes from an imaginary cigar in her fingers. "Does it count to have had *friends* who were *animals*.?"

"Oh, Kincaid. Really." But she smiled. It was one of the things she liked about her roommate: this insistence on the physical, her insistence on enjoying herself and on people enjoying her. Kincaid took everything seriously, even her humor. Only the truth, she said, could make you laugh. Unless it made you cry. Lies just make you angry. Or should.

"I love her, too, Angel," she said, scratching one of the cat's inflated ears, the knob that always raised the purr volume. Kincaid couldn't keep her mouth from curling at one end. "Sorry she nearly lost her surly little ass."

One hardly threatening fist raised, Elizabeth sat up making slightly spastic boxing motions toward Kincaid. "Are you emphasizing *sorry* or *nearly*?"

"Afraid I'll have to take the Fifth on that," Kincaid said, snatching her hand away from the cat, whose claws had sensed a patronizing attitude. "On occasion, consume one. Want some wine, Elizabeth?"

An admonishing frown ironed Elizabeth's face. "Not *this* early. *Some* of us have to work today." She looked at the cat and the crooning tone returned to her voice as she hoisted the animal to her shoulder and stood. "Come on, Amelia. Poor ole cowgirl's had such a bad day."

As she followed Kincaid down the hall and through the house, Elizabeth felt again the same sense of comfort and serenity she had intended when she furnished her house. She had chosen the warmth and quiet of teal and burgundy and soft lights and ferns and oriental things, books everywhere and furniture that wanted your company. Kincaid liked rooms a little livelier and had said so when she moved in, but her things didn't seem to contrast with Elizabeth's as much as complete them.

Kincaid tooled through the kitchen, picked up a wine decanter and sailed out to the pool. She had downed two glasses of Chablis before she noticed Elizabeth's warning look.

"Last one. Promise." Kincaid replenished her wine and stoppered the cut glass decanter, trying to ignore her friend's scolding though beautiful eyes. Kincaid loved to drink and did so often despite Elizabeth's policing. Although she realized there were healthier ways to do it, high priced spirits were the quickest way she knew to silence the chatter in her head and free the right side of her brain from its overbearing neighbor lobe. She did some of her best legal work when insights were free to occur.

She and Elizabeth sat by the pool in the shade, Elizabeth holding Amelia and a glass of something perfectly useless as far as Kincaid was concerned: Perrier water. "Naturally sparkling," it bubbled superfluously in two languages. Designer water that's pumped full of earth farts is more like it, Kincaid thought.

"All I'm saying, Elizabeth, is it will take forever for the University to clean up its act on its own. They know they're not paying people fairly. They've known it for years. People do what they want to do, as you've said so often." She took a sip of wine to let her words soak in a little. "A law suit would help every woman there and probably a lot of the men. Your case is classic, documented and allows those bastards not one iota of defensible ground."

They had had one version or another of this conversation a thousand times, but neither seemed to tire of finding new translations.

"You're the crusader, Kincaid, not me. This isn't a cause. It's just the principle of the thing."

"What's the difference?" Kincaid smiled; Elizabeth contradicted herself so infrequently that when she did, the flustered look that fleeted across her eyes always tickled the lawyer in Kincaid.

Elizabeth pretended to ignore the question, but she knew Kincaid had seen that look in her eyes. "Crusades need financing as well as principles. And you've always had the money. Half the cases you take can't pay you, so it's just as well you don't need the money."

An old thorn. "I don't owe anyone apologies for inheriting money from my parents or my practice from my father. He worked damned hard for it and so do I. Needing the work is not the same as needing the money." She knew she was getting a little too huffy, so she shut up and sucked on her wine.

"Oh, Kincaid, come on," Elizabeth said softly. "I don't want to argue. I'm just tired. Today's been a long week. OK?"

Kincaid hesitated a moment, reluctant to give up a pout she had worked so hard for. But she shrugged and nodded. She enjoyed a good mad sometimes, especially with Elizabeth, where it was so safe. But she enjoyed Elizabeth in a good mood even more, and laughing was preferable to almost anything. Almost. She shifted in her chair and changed the subject a degree or two.

"I don't see how you put up with a nimnul like Curtis, anyway." Kincaid had a thesaurus full of strange words for people she didn't admire: nimnuls, slobics, nurdettes, dilberts, republicans.

"It's easy. I ignore the pecking order until I feel a beak in my back. Then I look up a recipe for fricassee."

Kincaid jumped up, assuming her William-Jennings-Bryan-on-a-stump routine, jowls flying. "Filthy anarchist! What would America *be* without such blesséd institutions as the pecking order for men and beauty contests for women? Why, there'd be pillage, plunder, two-hour lunches, flextime, the demise of the two-party system."

"Good God forbid," Elizabeth breathed in pretended horror, pressing the back of her hand to her forehead as if to succumb to the vapors. "You don't mean—"

"Yes!" Kincaid hissed ominously, raising the fickle forefinger of truth. "Democracy! That twisted, radical promise of our forebears!" She thought a moment and wiggled her eyebrows suggestively. "Forefoxes, too."

Kincaid loved to make Elizabeth laugh, loved the sound and the thought of it and spent half her time in its pursuit. This time, though, her friend's amusement didn't last very long; pensiveness instead pressed its way back into Elizabeth's eyes.

"You know," she said softly, "understanding the reason for something is supposed to help a person deal with the thing itself." Elizabeth scratched Amelia, but the cat remained insistently unimpressed by attempts at establishing relationships as speculative as cause and effect. "Take the pecking order. For most people, all that amounts to is the appearance of power, pretended order. People who abuse those strategies come out of fear and insecurity, not strength." She stopped a second and smiled. "But I'd be a bit hard pressed to mourn Hitler's sad childhood while dancing to the ovens to help him feel a little more secure."

"Curtis is the one with the match to your pilot light."

"He's not dangerous. He's where he is by being penciled in on a rough draft of a preliminary organizational chart that somebody took seriously. He knows that he knows nothing about what I do. And he knows better than to interfere with my work."

"So? He still controls the budget, Elizabeth. The hand that rocks the calculator is the hand that rules the world."

"You know how I feel about working there. It's just, well, the students I see have such potential. It's not that I think I'm irreplaceable; I just want to make a difference. And there's the security." She took the cat's head in both hands and spoke directly to her. "Ameilia, remind the lady this is old material."

"Security?" Kincaid ignored the protest against redundancy. "That's the institutional cosmic joke. The University provides no security. Anybody can find any reason to fire anybody anytime. *You* are your only security. With a little help from your friends," she said, pointing to herself. "And from your friends," she said pointing to heaven.

"When'd you get *your* degree in psychology?" Elizabeth said.

Kincaid stuck her tongue out and dipped her fingers in her wine, flicking a shower toward Elizabeth. Most of it landed on Amelia, who did her best if-looks-could-kill number on Kincaid and leaped to the ground, shaking one foot at a time to dislodge either her bandages or the wine, whichever came first. "She's been watching Michael Jackson videos again," Kincaid laughed pointing to Amelia. Then she saw Elizabeth slowly empty her ice cubes on the ground and dip her glass in the pool, her dark eyes full of devilment.

"Slowly I turned," Elizabeth chanted, the glass raised in one hand, her other clinched into a talon. "Step, by step," she hissed, creeping not so stealthily toward Kincaid, who saw her fate in Elizabeth's eyes. She had seen it there often. Kincaid squealed like the sorority pledge she'd once been and jumped from her chair, ducking skillfully under Elizabeth's talon hand and poking her in the ribs playfully as she darted toward the kitchen door. "Last tag," Kincaid yelped, knowing she was just out of range, and thinking she might save herself, she took Amelia hostage and held her close.

"Dirty rat!" Elizabeth sloshed after her, then hesitated. She knew Amelia couldn't take a joke. "Dirty rat," she sang and even as she sang, she laughed. Through her mind flashed a scene when she was four years old, and that name had been flung at her from the slingshot lips of some boy. For some inexplicable reason, the epithet had stunned her to paralysis and impotency. Probably because at four, her vocabulary didn't provide anything equally devastating with which to lay him out. Funny how words lost their power to time. Or to other words.

* * *

"She's too fast for you, Fred," Chuck said, peering into Curtis' office and beyond him to the track out the window.

"Huh?" Curtis had been looking out his window at the late afternoon runners and at the particularly attractive and agile woman lapping the less serious joggers on the track outside his office. Actually, Curtis had only been watching with half a brain; his other half wrestled with the intricacies of the budget printout he held in his hand. "Huh?" Curtis said again.

"Her." Chuck pointed out the window to the runner. "She's too fast for you." Chuck smiled, but whatever wit he had intended was lost on Curtis, who stared blankly at him a moment, then back down at the printout. Curtis punched some buttons on his calculator and looked at the resulting figures as though they'd just been beamed to him from Mars.

"I think you ought to look at this, Fred." Chuck had come in with a manila folder in his hand, and he extended it now toward the older man and waited for Curtis to disentangle himself from the dot matrix on his desk.

Curtis opened the folder and looked absently at the first page as Chuck closed Curtis' office door. Within a few seconds, Curtis' bored expression changed to confusion and then recognition and suspicion. Snapping the folder shut, he glared at Chuck and thrust the papers toward the younger man.

"Lizbuth's notes on her clients are confidential, Chuck! *You* shouldn't have these! And what the hell are you showing them to *me* for?"

"They're copies," Chuck said calmly. "They won't be missed."

"Jesus, Chuck! What the hell are you doing? Do you know how much trouble this—?"

"*She's* trouble already, Fred," Chuck interrupted and tapped the folder. "There's your answer. Read it."

Curtis opened his mouth to respond, but nothing came out as he looked from Chuck to the folder and back again. Tentatively, he opened the cover, wondering as he did if Pandora's problems had been crated in manila. He read, slowly at first, then picked up speed, but things continued to make no sense to him. He saw no connection between this and any of his problems, and the faster he read, the angrier he got. He snapped the folder shut again and looked diliberately at Chuck.

"Now that you've made me—" he hesitated, angrily searching for the right word but selecting something close but no cigar, "an *accomplish*, would you mind telling me the *point*." His words were clipped at the edges by the sharp blades of impatience

Surely he can't be that dense, Chuck thought. But he saw no hint of understanding in Curtis. "You can stop Elizabeth with that, Fred." He took the folder from Fred's hand.

"With what?" Fred was trying not to shout.

"Fred, listen," Chuck said slowly, keeping his own impatience in check. "The legal office is on our case, right?" Fred merely stared at him. "You don't know where to get the money to raise Elizabeth's salary, much less Tony's and David's. My father says Paul Thompson is a very tight man with a dollar, even tighter with another man who isn't."

Curtis started to flare. "Don't tell me what I—!"

"Fred, just *listen*. I'm trying to help."

Curtis' jaw clenched and his eyes narrowed, but he shut up. Chuck walked across the room and sat on the couch, secure now with his own point advantage.

"Elizabeth's pretty cocky, you know. From the way she acts, she must think her job's pretty safe here. But maybe," he said, opening the folder and flipping the pages slowly, pointedly, "just maybe, a case could be made, to her at least, that her position isn't, well, as safe as she thinks."

An angry blank stare met him when he looked up. The thought skidded through Chuck's head that Thompson had put him with this man as some kind of very unfunny joke on his father. He blinked it away and concentrated on the task at hand, which seemed to consist of remedial thinking. Take it slow. One plod at a time, he thought.

"Look, Fred. Elizabeth isn't married, is she? I've checked around. She lives with a woman. Both over thirty." His voice trailed off and he watched an ember of understanding begin to smoke in Curtis' eye.

"What are you inferring to me?"

How'd he get through graduate school with this advanced case of malapropism? Chuck took another breath. "Implying, Fred," he said before he could edit himself. "This Lisa Hunter is a lesbian. I'd stake my degree on it. I talked to Elizabeth about it. Twice. You should hear her. She won't even discuss it. *Very* defensive about it. Says *I'm* wrong. But here in her own notes, her own handwriting, she as much as *agrees*. Now, maybe . . . maybe she has some, well, *personal* reason to. . . ."

The spark caught in the wind, and realization spread across the plane of Curtis' face. "You mean accuse Lizbuth of being *queer*?" Then he started to laugh. "Are you *kidding*? *Lizbuth*?!" He walked over to Chuck, still laughing and took the folder from him and laid it on his desk. "You don't even know her, Chuck. She practically lives with Tony Scalla. This is ridiculous."

"I don't have to know her, Fred. *I* don't believe it's *true*! It doesn't have to be true, don't you see? Nobody can fight that kind of accusation. That's the beauty of it. You don't have to prove anything. Just *say* it. *Imply* it."

"On the *basics* of *this*?" Randomly inappropriate words were bubbling up on the heat of Curtis' anger. "I'm not even supposed to have *seen* this shit!"

"You don't use that, Fred. You use the *knowledge* of it." He saw Curtis waver slightly and pressed his point. "You don't go public with this stuff. You just make *her* see that her position here might not be, well, worth quite what she thinks it is."

Curtis rocked back in his chair, pensively rapping his knuckles on the folder and the opportunities inside. But whipping out of nowhere, a sojourning conscience landed a reluctant blow. Almost on its own, his left hand flicked the offending sheaf across the desk toward Chuck. "Get rid of this thing!" Curtis breathed.

Chuck stood slowly and walked to the desk to pick up his attempt. He tapped it against the knuckles of this other hand like the ticking of an old clock in need of winding.

"You've only got until Monday, Fred. Sorry I couldn't help." He shrugged and walked to the door, still tapping with his hand. He opened the door and stepped into the hall where he heard the roar of Martha's laughter, punctuated on every inhalation with a loud snort. As he came down the hall he could hear Elizabeth in the midst of some cat story. Privately, he thought these stories were entertaining, but Martha and Tony were usually her sole audience, and he had only heard snatches. Martha was about to fall off her chair, not from the content of the story so much as the way Elizabeth could somehow make you believe she was the animal under discussion. Elizabeth had her back to him as he approached the empty reception area.

"This labrador was this big, Martha." Elizabeth measured to her waist. "But he's obviously untrained in the social graces. Now, my cat is registered as a conscientious objector. She even moved to Canada in the sixties. But she just got fed up with that dog's patronizing attitude. So she gave it one of these actions—"

Just as Chuck and his misappropriated documents arrived at Elizabeth's side, she brought her arm around in a sweeping imitation of a feline slash. She caught the folder square in its center and launched it toward the middle of the room, its contents fluttering around like so many startled chickens. The startled rooster, so recently in charge of the coop, fluttered after them, his eyes about the same circumference as his mouth.

"Oh, no," stammered Elizabeth, embarrassed and apologetic as she rushed to help clean up the mess she'd made. She stooped and grasped a sheet as Chuck reached for it. He grabbed her wrist. And none too gently.

"No! That's all right, Elizabeth! I'll get it, I'll get it!" Chuck squeezed her arm more fiercely than he was aware, and it was that that got her attention. He dropped the sheet he had as he reached for hers, but she took it in her other hand, perturbed by his grip and suspicious.

Glancing at the paper, she instantly recognized her own handwriting. His face was becoming a neutral mask, but he still had hold of her arm. Her face tensed from suspicion to anger. With measured firmness, she twisted her arm toward his thumb and popped easily loose from his grasp. Red marks circled her skin like a bracelet. She continued to look at the sheet in her hand. Slowly, her head followed her eyes as they locked on Chuck's pupils.

"How did you get this?" Her voice was even and quiet, a sure sign to Martha that all the goonies in Hades were soon to be loosed on the world, or at least on Chuck.

Chuck seemed to be ignoring her as he calmly bent and retrieved the other sheets on the floor. Then he straightened and sedately stacked them inside their cover.

"I asked you a question, Chuck." Now her jaw tightened. Martha was in heaven.

"Just calm down, Elizabeth." Chuck sounded like he thought he was talking to a child, or a client, both of whom received the same tone. "If you want to discuss this, come to my office."

"We'll discuss it right here." Her diction had become impeccable, with every consonant rapier edged.

Chuck smiled, of all things, and patted her on the shoulder. What a Christian, Martha thought. She wasn't thinking of Chuck.

"I'm not going to talk to you while you're being irrational," Chuck continued. "And *not* in front of Martha."

"You could write notes to one another, Chuck," Martha offered. "I can't read your writing."

Only the slightest movement of his eyelids indicated he had even heard Martha, and he continued to look at Elizabeth as she folded the sheet in her hand and creased it twice. "I'll be in my office. *When* you calm down," Chuck said and turned with enormous manufactured serenity and strode down the corridor to his office with Elizabeth firing volleys at his back with her eyes.

Her anger had now turned to incredulousness as she looked from the empty hallway to the sheet in her hand, thoughts forming. Then she looked in the opposite direction to Curtis' door. "Chuck just came out of Fred's office. With this in his hand."

"He went in there with that folder while you were standing here," Martha said. "I doubt his purpose was to deliver office supplies." Martha was as mad as Elizabeth and less likely to attempt empathy.

Down the hall, Curtis' door opened, and he emerged into the invisibly chaotic air swirling silently around him. Head down and unsmiling, he trudged toward the two women. In his hand he carried a scruffy briefcase with only one functioning latch, threatening hourly to disgorge semi-secrets of semi-state to the eager smog of day. He was on his way to see Paul Thompson, and he was not happy. He looked up at the two women staring at him and, unable to read history from their expressions, flashed them his best imitation of a smile.

"Martha, I'll be in meetings all afternoon so I won't be back until Monday and I'll be out of town fishing this weekend. I'll bring you a trout." Martha detested fish, but he could never remember, so he always brought her one: scales, head and all.

He looked at Elizabeth and smiled.

"How's the world treatin' ya, Lizbuth?" He patted her arm as he flowed past her and floated out of the office and out of sight. He both knew and did not know the answer to his question. And what that amounted to was refusing to learn.

Elizabeth stared at the empty doorway with sin in her heart. Then she glowered down the hall in Chuck's direction, the possibilities for a life of crime listing themselves in her head along with various epithets that described the dubious legitimacy of Chuck's lineage.

"Martha," she said in her softest, angriest voice, her jaw muscles pulsating, "Hold my calls. I'm going down to Dr. Gardner's office to see if I can calm down."

It wasn't what Chuck had done that infuriated her. She didn't know what he'd done. She was furious, but she wanted to make sure she was justified in her murderous intent. She'd wait until she had the facts before she would allow herself to feel righteous indignation as well. She always felt everybody deserved the benefit of the doubt, although she often gave it through gritted teeth. (Kincaid told Elizabeth that the world would reap better rewards if she would give the Benefit of the Doubt as a non-profit organization fundraiser.) No, it was Chuck's infernal, unwarranted receiver-of-the-stone-tablets attitude that lit her fuse. And because she could feel mendacity swirling through the air as if it were mustard gas.

She knocked once on Chuck's door, turned the knob simultaneously and stepped into this office.

He looked up from his desk and forged an unpleasant smile. "I'm busy right now, Elizabeth. Could this wait?" He meant it as a statement not open to debate.

"I don't think so, Chuck." She stared narrowly at him, her voice level. "Confidentiality is not something I need more time to form an opinion on. What were you doing with copies of my notes on Lisa?"

He might as well have patted her on the head or tweaked her cheek. "You don't seem to have calmed down enough to listen to anything I might have to say." His mind raced for something that would stall her.

She drew in a long, slow breath and narrowed her eyes even further. He looked back down at the papers on his desk and picked up a pen, wiping the tiniest amount of sweat from his upper lip. She stepped toward his desk, reached across it and put her palm down on the paper at which he so intently stared.

She swiveled her palm and the paper under it. "It would help your comprehension level if you turned this right side up to read it."

His jaw tensed and he gave her a sharp look as he pushed himself back from his desk and stood.

"Answer my question, Chuck. I don't want to have to talk to Fred about this."

"That's exactly who you'll have to talk to. He gave the notes to me." Chuck walked to the door and opened it. "You may not be busy, but I am. Dr. Curtis will have to answer your questions. I'm not at liberty to discuss them."

She glared at him a moment before going out the door. Then she turned and said evenly, "I hope that he can resolve this. But you and I, Chuck, have other things on the agenda. Not the least of which is your attitude. And mine."

He knew that his look of consumate disdain was his most devastating to opponents, and he conjured it up just before closing the door. But in his office alone, all haughtiness drained from his face as he sank into his chair and ran both hands through his thick blond hair. It was Elizabeth's fault that he was in this mess to begin with. Why she had to cause such an uproar about her salary was beyond him. The woman had no concept of how to play on a team; she only thought of herself. The rules were that you took what you were offered and didn't ask questions. Then you out-maneuvered and out-flanked and out-gunned the people around you to get what you wanted. It also burned him that Elizabeth didn't seem impressed by anything he had to offer, didn't need him at all. But it burned deep in the hollow of his consciousness where he was only aware of the heat and not the light.

He had not had time to think about what had happened in the reception area and was so shaken by being caught that he had said the only thing that had come into his head. You never blamed anything on a supervisor, and you certainly never lied about them: Lies and blame, like orders and shit, were subject to the laws of gravity: They only flowed downhill. But he had the weekend to make the puzzle fit the answer. He'd saved his ass before, he could save it again.

* * *

Paul Thompson had been at the University longer than God. There were even those who hinted that God had often been called by others to assist him, but that Thompson had refused the help as being a duplication of effort. Not conceit, as he would say, just accurate self-assessment. The

Vice President for Finance and Development had an unbelievable genius for knowing where every penny at the University came from and where each of them went and through whose hands. Always and forever. And like most people who can't teach or be good parents, he could not fathom a mind which was not a duplicate of his own.

He had infinite patience with everything and everyone as long as the subject wasn't money. It took a great deal of convincing, however, for him to believe that anything or anyone was free of the connection. Cheap, maybe, but not free.

Nobody ever volunteered for a meeting with him to discuss their own budget. Unless it was in the context of getting money out of somebody else's. So he knew why Curtis was coming when his secretary told him of the appointment. He ran the tape of Curtis' budget history in his head and knew the answer would be no before Curtis waddled into his office.

Thompson could not abide people with sloppy middles or sloppy minds, and here, as if God had created Curtis specifically to irritate him, this man had both. Thompson skimmed through the papers that Curtis had been belaboring him with for an hour and looked up over the sheets and his half-lens glasses at the sweating insect before him.

Curtis picked up something else that had just slid from his crowded lap, or what passed for one, and smiled weakly.

"*You* prepared this request for a budget increase?" Thompson asked rhetorically.

Curtis nodded and dropped something else.

If I could find this man amusing or even entertaining, Thompson thought, maybe he wouldn't exhaust me so. "I don't see any explanation for these figures, Curtis. Page four, item six. What's *that* five thousand for?"

Damn, Curtis thought as he rifled through the papers in his lap. He expects you to memorize this shit. What's the point of writing anything down? Can't he read? He's got his own damn copies of the breakdown.

Thompson waited an eternity. At least three seconds. "If you don't know what it's for, it can't be very important, can it." Thompson twisted his gold Cross pen and drew an eradicating line through the mystery. Then, for effect, he seemed to consider the rest of the figures for a moment and finally twisted his pen again, rendering it and further discussion pointless.

Curtis sat with his mouth open, realizing after a few moments of awkward silence that the meeting had been adjourned without a second to the motion. Slowly, unable to keep the dejected look from his eyes, he began to cram his papers back into his briefcase.

Thompson thrived on dejected eyes. They meant he'd done his job and located another bottom line, bottomer than anyone had expected. Dejected eyes made him happy, and suddenly he felt almost congenial toward this poor wretch. The man wasn't so bad. After all, he did what he was told, tried hard, was always on time. And he would be perfect training for Gardner's boy. If Gardner's boy could succeed with this man in his way, he could do anything.

"How's Chuck Gardner coming along, Curtis?" Thompson said, neither needing nor expecting a response.

"Well . . . he's got some things to learn—"

"Good, good." Thompson wasn't listening. "Need to keep him on the fast track if he's good enough. I beat his dad out for first string tailback one year, you know." He smiled, remembering the look on Gardner's face decades ago when the squad list had been posted their junior year. "He never did get over that. But we have to keep the ole boy happy now. Rich alumni don't grow in the botany building, ha-ha."

Jesus, thought Curtis. Only a card-carrying asshole laughs like that. I mean actually laughs *ha-ha* like that, like he was reading it or something. And only a card-carrying asshole would enjoy putting me in this bind. I wouldn't ask him for the goddamn money if I didn't need it. Damn it. Should have padded the thing by ten thousand. Should have known he'd screw me over.

His throat felt as dry as a one hump camel on a two hump desert. He was glad he didn't have to endure Martha being pleasant another hour or his wife being fat another night, not when there was the alternative of liquid amnesia right across the street.

* * *

Curtis looked up from his third Bourbon to see who the hell this guy was who couldn't hold his liquor and who had bumped into his table, nearly making him spill his own. But he recognized the face through the fumes of alcohol and smoke and flashed a dimly lit drinking-buddy grin like fog covered neon.

"Hey, Williams! You ole rat's ass!" Curtis slurred, though not racially.

Williams peered beyond his nose, and with gargantuan effort, willed his eyes into focus. Curtis' face shimmied into his consciousness.

"Hey, Curtis," he said, without much enthusiasm or many consonants. John Williams had been at the University longer than Curtis. They had a lot in common, shared common histories, common views. Straight bourbon, straight Republican tickets, straight faces on the straight and narrow. Curtis liked the word *straight*. It was clean, tight, sharp. Damn straight.

"Sit down," Curtis said loudly. "Lemme buy ya one."

"You can buy me six if you want." Williams drifted into the chair across from Curtis and nonverbaled his order to a waitress as he sank. "We can call it . . . a . . . retirement party. Yeah. That's it. Retirement." His face fell like an old prune and draped around the hand that supported his head.

God, thought Curtis. He's looking old. "Retirement?" He flinched at the word. "You're nowhere near retirement, John. You're younger than I am."

Williams raised his glass to his lips and said over the rim, "The University's letting me go, Fred." His voice was hollow, empty, echoing in his ears, the glass a cavern.

"What?" A knot formed in Curtis' throat and slipped to his stomach.

"Go, Fred. Letting me go," he enunciated slowly. "Watch my lips. Seems we've got a bad case of the Insufficients. Insufficient publications, insufficient students, insufficient funds. They're calling it early retirement, but I know better. Thought we were immune, didn't we, Fred? Knew where all the bodies were buried." He gulped another slug of whiskey.

"You know where more bodies are than I do, John," Curtis said weakly.

"Then better pray your skeletons are buried with treasure. Nothing counts anymore but money. God help you if you start to cost them."

Curtis heard a sound like nails being driven into a coffin and realized that it was his heart pounding.

* * *

The door slamming sounded like a cannon and almost choked the cat. Amelia had been indulging in her favorite owner-harassing activity: grazing on the palms and ferns in Elizabeth's living room. Sitting in the lush greenery under the watchful, but totally useless eyes of a life-size cast iron Doberman, Amelia had just taken a small helpless frond between her delicate little liver lips, having long ago discovered that this sculpted canine sentinal on whose feet she sat might smell like a fire hydrant, but it didn't act in the least bit doggy, so she was safe in her perverted palm pursuits. When Elizabeth had first put the metal dog in amongst the plants, Amelia had merely smiled to herself at Elizabeth's naivete. Amelia was not to be kept from her grazing and certainly not by an imitation dog. Humans were so quaint. They thought that because they could speak, they were bright. Telepathy was the real talent, and Amelia had to admit that both her humans were better at it than most.

But the door slamming not only sounded like a cannon, it fired the cat clear across the room like a mini ball. She ricocheted off three corner moldings and a silk flower arrangement before regaining her sense of due North as she castaneted down the hall and under a bed.

Kincaid peered warily around the corner at Elizabeth, winner of the ten meter free style door slam, who was stalking around the living room, rewinding the day's events under her breath.

"Curtis again?" Kincaid undid the bath towel around her to rewrap it tighter.

"Close," Elizabeth spat. "How'd you guess?"

"The cat always knows when to hide."

"Then she'd better hide twice," she hissed. "Curtis has an apprentice now: *Doctor* Gardner." She was still stomping around the room, making a trail of little spiked heel dents in the oriental carpet. "That sneaking, arrogant, overbearing, under-educated insufferable twit! Both of them!" Elizabeth used the word *twit* when she really meant *sonofabitch*. She hated the system that assigned no epithets directly to men, only to their mother, thus rendering men implicitly innocent, their behavior preventable or at least capable of remediation had their mothers only behaved better and not given birth.

Kincaid knew better than to venture into the path of this little tornado and stayed in the doorway, her long, dark, wet hair making little rivers down her back. And she knew better than to support Elizabeth in her anger with a Damn Right or a Sue The Bastards paragraph, because then Elizabeth would stop being mad, which she probably had a right to be, and start defending all the hitherto aforementioned insufferable twits.

"Some wine and aspirin might help," Kincaid offered softly.

"A twelve-gauge sawed-off *shotgun* might *help!*"

"How about one brilliant lawyer and a small multi-billion dollar law suit?"

Elizabeth sighed and looked at Kincaid, and she allowed a small, tired smile. "That'll do, I guess. If it comes with wine and aspirin."

"Indeed, m'lady. And a hot bath already drawn. We have two whole hours before we are due at Dr. Harrison's, so you have until eight to explore your *Angst*." She said the last word with a face and Nazi accent that would give you some if you didn't already have any.

"I don't have *Angst*, Kincaid. I have latent homocidal tendencies."

Elizabeth had already begun discarding her clothes as she moved past Kincaid, who watched each piece fall into a trail perhaps intended to help Gretel find her way back to Bloomingdale's. She watched Elizabeth's naked form disappear into the bathroom, threw up her hands in resignation and picked up the trail, piece by piece, and followed her into the steam.

"Do me a favor, Elizabeth. Whatever it's about at work, please don't get off on it tonight with Dr. Harrison. You two start talking about school, and I may as well slip into a coma."

Elizabeth stepped into the tub, closed her eyes and slid slowly into the water, blue waves closing silently over her head as she sank. I'm just not going to think about it, she thought, not any of it. I'm going to take the weekend off and not think. It's my birthday tomorrow. I shouldn't have to think on my very own birthday. Oh, Melanie, Melanie, Ah can bahly get these hoop skirts thru this dowah.

* * *

PART IV

Dinner at the professor's was like receiving the Nobel prize: Very few were considered for the honor and fewer still were actually invited. This was only the third time Kincaid and Elizabeth had been dubbed. It was an event of such import that it even succeeded in getting Kincaid to get ready on time. Somewhere in her heritage was a little Cherokee, and she blamed her having her own personal time zone on that particular unruly gene.

For years, Dr. Harrison had been one of those exasperating individuals who got everything to the dinner table at the correct temperature, in the correct serving dish that matched in pattern everything else, on time and simultaneously.

"Amazing," said Elizabeth to their hostess of this event when it was over.

"No," Dr. Harrison smiled, "unnatural. Being on time is the most unnatural thing in the universe. The seasons vary, if only by a minute or two; the tides change their schedule. The moon may be on a twenty-eight day cycle, but she doesn't wear a Rolex to do it. She'd just as soon be full during the day as the middle of the night. No," she said almost wistfully, "we just strap on watches and insist there be order in the world when basically there is none."

"There's order," said Kincaid. "It's just not linear. Surely a man invented the clock. It wouldn't have occurred to a woman that other creatures didn't already know what time it was."

"I think we should have some brandy, if we're going to decry the patriarchy." Dr. Harrison folded her napkin. "That task requires liquor to numb the senses."

The three women packed up and moved to Dr. Harrison's study, which seemed to have been collecting everything but dust for thirty years. Kincaid found something new to look at everytime she went in there. Along the walls were dark oil paintings and antique doodads among the hundreds of books and photographs and leather bound volumes that Dr. Harrison had herself authored.

"Well," Kincaid said, pointing to an autographed photograph of the professor with some well-known civil rights marchers, "you've been decrying the patriarchy longer than I have. You were one of the first to do more than just speak out on this particular Ism. You put your life on the line in those marches." Dr. Harrison prided herself on her financial and vocal support of almost every liberal issue, although the closer the issue came to home, the quieter she became, the more likely it was that she use covert maneuvering than frontal assault. In that sense she was extremely conservative. Self preservation dictated the wisdom of using projectiles before wrestling.

Another piece of wisdom that hung on her wall was a parchment copy of the Bill of Rights.

Kincaid smiled. "I'm still amazed when I hear that some Americans have never even read this. Did you know that during the Bicentennial some guy went to a mall and asked people to sign a petition that said they supported these things? That's all that was on it: just the first Ten Amendments. Half the people refused to sign because they thought it was a communist plot. The other half were afraid it was part of an entrapment scheme by the FBI."

"Actually," Dr. Harrison said seriously, "it was divinely inspired. No document since the New Testament has so exhorted mankind to get over its baser self."

Elizabeth chuckled. "How'd the part about bearing arms slip in there then?"

"It's all in the interpretation," said Kincaid. "They were talking about sleeveless dresses."

"No wonder the men in the mall were upset," Dr. Harrison said. "Not many men like wearing sleeveless dresses."

Kincaid glanced slyly at Elizabeth. "But that's why the Constitution was written to begin with. So that those few who are into sleeveless frocks could indulge themselves."

Kincaid inspected another photograph, older yet, of a much younger Dr. Harrison, a young man and another young woman. The man stood in the middle with one arm around each woman. Neither woman looked as pleased as he, least of all the young Jeanette Harrison.

"This one of your mystery sweeties, Dr. H.?" Kincaid said teasingly, pointing toward the man.

Dr. Harrison laughed. She liked the way Kincaid felt relaxed around her, comfortable enough to take little verbal pokes. "He was a mystery all right, but not mine, thank heaven. The other . . . lady . . . is the one who gave him her life, fortune and sacred honor." Kincaid glanced at Elizabeth to see if she'd heard that little break in the older woman's voice. She had;

Elizabeth's eyes held a silent caution. They both knew that Dr. Harrison's history wasn't her own favorite subject.

"Didn't you ever think about it? Marriage, I mean?" Kincaid said cautiously.

Dr. Harrison swirled her brandy and watched the ocean design it made on the side of the snifter. "Oh, I suppose I did. When I was twenty-five or so and everyone else was doing it," She took a slow sip of the amber liquid and smiled. "But it's like hunger: If you wait long enough, the urge leaves you."

Well, there's thin and then there's anorexic, thought Kincaid, but she didn't say it. "I wish I'd had your patience. My scorecard read: Peer pressure, two; Kincaid, zip. Got married at twenty-two and by twenty-four, I was enlightened and divorced."

Dr. Harrison looked at Elizabeth. "I thought you said she had a lot of patience."

"She does. But not for things like waiting." Elizabeth's eyes twinkled, and Kincaid's tongue shot out like a lizard's toward a June bug.

In the doorway, Dr. Harrison spotted Dog, who sat expectantly asking to be invited to step on the prayer rug that covered the floor. When their eyes met, Dog's tail swept slowly in a little furry arc, and she did a down tempo tango with her front legs.

"Come on in, Fuzz Face. But don't ask for any brandy. And only one cigar. You know what the doctor said." Dr. Harrison sat on the couch and patted her leg. Dog ambled in like an old snail and sat leaning against the spot Dr. Harrison had patted. "May I get you more brandy, Kincaid?" Dr. Harrison said.

"Yes," Kincaid said in a breathy stage whisper, "but don't tell Elizabeth."

"I'm not her keeper," Elizabeth said, rolling her eyes at the eldest woman.

"Oh, yes she is, Dr. Harrison. She just doesn't like to admit it," Kincaid whispered loudly.

Dog's legs withdrew their support on ethical grounds, and she slid like a wet wall of mud into a pile of the floor.

"Can't stand a dog who can't hold her liquor," said Elizabeth, looking at Dog.

"*Well!*" Kincaid huffed indignantly. "And after I spent an hour on my hair."

Dr. Harrison chuckled and looked from one woman's face to the other. The look in their eyes as they smiled at each other was familiar, but like seeing a person out of her usual context, Dr. Harrison couldn't immediately identify it. From the wall behind Kincaid, the younger Dr. Harrison looked out from her static trio to the living three with unseeing eyes, as if from another dimension, moving at a different speed approaching light.

"Don't get up, Dr. Harrison. I'll bring the brandy over there," said

Kincaid, and she pointed her thumb at Elizabeth. "And we won't let *her* have any."

"I have a Christian name, Kincaid. I think you've known me long enough to use it," said Dr. Harrison.

Kincaid raised her glass in toast. "Daddy always told me it was proper to wait until invited or provoked beyond all reason before using anything but a surname. Madame name, I should have corrected him. While he was still correctable."

"Coulda, woulda, shoulda," Elizabeth said softly. "The subjunctive mood is responsible for more guilt and regret than organized religion."

"Organized religion," observed Kincaid dryly, "invented the subjunctive mood."

Elizabeth put her finger to her tongue and drew a tally in the air in front of her. But Kincaid couldn't tell the column heading under which the score had been recorded, so she changed the subject.

"I can't imagine living alone for . . . what? Forty years?" She looked at Dr. Harrison over her snifter. "After the second month, I'd have refused to listen when I talked to myself."

"It's not so bad. I have my writing. And my University, my students. And Dog." Dog flopped her tail once in response to her name, and locked eyes with Elizabeth, whose eyes looked very much like her own. Dog raised herself a millimeter and made two little lurches toward where Elizabeth sat.

"It will take her until the next decade, Elizabeth, but Dog is coming to see you." Dr. Harrison grinned. "Irrational fear of rejection." Dog scooted another inch.

"Shall I encourage her or let her do it her own way?"

"Always encourage. Always. But she'll do it her own way in spite of it."

"Come here, chubby slug," crooned Elizabeth. Dog snuck forward half a foot.

"She's my third one," Dr. Harrison said sadly, a distant look in her eyes. "I seem to outlive everything." She drifted momentarily, then seemed to pull herself back with effort and smiled. "Everything but my books and my work. Attempts at non-genetic immortality."

Elizabeth looked admiringly at the professor. "Your last book—all of them, for that matter—incredible. I've never read anyone who could make history so entertaining."

"There was one other critic who held a similar view. It's of some comfort to feel that I am not alone in my opinions." Her humility was playful and unnecessary.

"Your publisher seems to believe that you have an agreeing audience the size of the population of Southern California." Elizabeth watched Dog go through another Camp LeJeune training maneuver.

"Southern New Hampshire, I think," said Dr. Harrison. She stared at Elizabeth's striking profile, then down at her hands, turning and turning the brandy, now almost gone. A little too much tonight, she thought, and not like me at all. "I believe it's time," she breathed, almost to herself, then looked beside her at Kincaid, this darker beauty. "I have dark secrets, you see." Her voice was radio-melodrama ominous. "A world into which I disappear, where no one knows to look. I think I know you two well enough now to invite you in." She rose from her chair and started toward the stairway.

The two younger women glanced at each other, playfully suspicious.

"What about Dog?" said Elizabeth. "She's almost made it across the abyss."

"She'll get over it," Dr. Harrison laughed. "She's spent half her existence pursuing life from that position. Come on."

Up the stairs and down a long hall was Dr. Harrison's bedroom, though Elizabeth and Kincaid didn't know where they were being led. Legend had it that this stairway led to the twilight zone; no one in recent memory had ever been shown anything more than the banister.

Dr. Harrison opened her door and turned to them. "Wait here." Her voice was still a charade, and her eyes twinkled as she closed her bedroom door, leaving them in the hall.

In a second, the door opened a crack and her hand appeared holding gray and white striped train engineers' caps. Above the bill in red embroidery, each said "N.C. & St.L."

Kincaid looked at Elizabeth and mouthed, hardly audible, "*Kinky.*"

"Oh, shut up," Elizabeth said, so noiselessly as to be almost telepathic, but Kincaid knew she was fooling. Elizabeth took the caps and jammed one down over Kincaid's eyes. She set the other lightly on her own head and went in while Kincaid felt her way by Braille, tugging at the brim. She heard the noise before she could focus too well, and then she saw it.

One whole half of the enormous room was not a bedroom at all but a waist-high, miniature landscape. And between the tiny trees and towns, snaked an antique Lionel train. The real kind. The choo-choo kind. A time machine.

It *was* the twilight zone. Suddenly all three of them were seven years old, little girls dancing and jockeying for the controls, looking for things to fill and empty. A world to run and order. Dr. Harrison cocked her chief engineer's hat rakishly and tooted her unique approach-warning horn-howl that she had played for such long and solitary hours that it was like something that belonged to Bessie Smith.

"I've allowed very few people to play in here," she shouted over the noise of the engine. "I trust you two will take note of that singular honor. I am speaking of enormous responsibility here, ladies."

Laughing up at her, Elizabeth watched Kincaid fiddling with everything within reach to see if and how it worked and sat on the edge of the book-covered four-poster, dislodging one of the volumes. Stepping back for a better view, Kincaid tripped on the book and stooped to examine the impediment.

Her back to them, Dr. Harrison huddled over her controls to her patch of earth as Kincaid raised the book by its spine. The old volume of Millay's poetry seemed like a portrait of its owner, the polished, dark ridges of leather shining against the gold inlaid printing and gilded pages, the pages yellow with turning, remembering. Something, a page marker of some kind, slipped from the book and floated to the floor.

Kincaid picked up the marker curiously, looking from it to the professor, then at Elizabeth. She handed the book and its marker to her friend on the bed.

Elizabeth looked at the old photograph once torn in half, now repaired carefully and touched either less often or more reverently than the pages it measured. It framed two women's young faces: Jeanette and Our Lady of Sacred Honor, the woman whose photograph they had seen downstairs. And these eyes spoke only to each other. But they shouted silently to Elizabeth down a forty-year passage with a message that would require blindness to miss.

She closed the book, held it cradled in her lap and glanced at Kincaid. The young woman next to her touched one finger to her forehead above her mythical third eye and indicated Dr. Harrison with the two she normally used. It was a sign between them, a code, that one of them might have found another friend, a sister. Someone who might speak the same language or possibly not need words at all.

"Where'd you two go?" Dr. Harrison called over her shoulder. "I can't run this thing alone. Well, I can, but it's no fun," she laughed as she tooted the whistle and glanced at Elizabeth. Her eyes softened as they fell to the book in her lap. "You take the throttle, Kincaid. I've almost made the track too complicated," she puffed, but Kincaid didn't need to be overly encouraged. "Don't run her too fast, though, She's old."

"She's beautiful. And I'll bet she's stronger than you think," Kincaid saw the smiling caution in the older woman's eyes. "I won't wreck her, I promise," said said, a little kid again.

Dr. Harrison sat next to Elizabeth, both of them laughing at the newly hired engineer. "This must be your favorite book, Jeanette."

"It is. How could you tell?"

"Telepathy," Elizabeth smiled. "Not really. It's like my students' blue jeans. You can always tell their favorite pair by the way they fit and the amount of blue still left in them."

Elizabeth handed her the book as Dr. Harrison looked back at Kincaid and laughed at the mouth hex that Kincaid had conjured to help the train around a curve. Had it not been for that soft little pointed tongue caught between her teeth, surely centrifugal force would have triumphed over purpose. Dr. Harrison didn't know all the laws of physics, but she suspected that where centrifugal force was concerned, a little magic was essential. She wrapped her arms softly around Millay, the book pressed close to her, rocking gently, gently in small and soothing efforts. But smiling still. And conjuring unaware.

"Happy birthday, Elizabeth," she said.

* * *

She didn't know what tribe had come through town for her birthday, but they had brought an Indian summer with them and left the hottest part of it for Elizabeth as a surprise. So her crowd had drug out their bathing suits one more time with feeling and were standing and dancing around her pool, tastefully undressed for one last day before hibernation set in with a vengeance.

They also came because they didn't want to miss anything. Lines would be invented here that would be quoted all year long and all over town. Dishing as a second language relied on a distinction between direct and indirect objects, subjects and predicates; those absent were likely to become an unchosen part of speech.

Across a sea of beautifully bare bodies in bathing suits and shorts and men's bikinis, Elizabeth could hear Tony delivering his favorite joke to a small crowd, some of whom he didn't know. David Stein and his wife Kathy had been hauled into the audience for body count.

"There's this drag queen, see," said Tony, launching into his best camp act, which was difficult since he looked like he ought to be hauling logs somewhere in Oregon. "And it's her first time in a Catholic church. She's never seen the Easter parade with all the little priests and acolytes. And she's just *real* impressed. And then here comes this major motion priest down the aisle, all done up in his *finer* long robe and beads. And he's swinging this smoking incense burner in front of him, doncha know." Tony paused to take a sip of his wine. "Well . . . the drag queen reaches out and tugs at the priest's sleeve and says in her most *discreet* voice: '*Love* your dress, Loretta! But your purse is on fire.' "

As expected, three people roared and four groaned at a story that never seemed to complete the rounds. There was always someone young or new to listen.

"The priest, of course," said David, "was incensed." Then the groaning began in earnest. Groaning at puns was obligatory in this circle.

It was a circle in which almost everyone knew each other; they'd all been coming to either Elizabeth's or Tony's or Kincaid's for years. When Kincaid had moved in with Elizabeth five years before, her entourage had merged with Elizabeth's even though parts of both already overlapped. It was a strangely eclectic group who collectively couldn't fit comfortably inside a single category, although they had convinced themselves that they did: They all loved hardwood floors and oriental carpets. The joint ownership of the hardwoods changed, the partners changed, but the dance never did. New dancers were added from year to year until this specially charged nucleus of people numbered near seventy-five. But this was just Elizabeth's particular molecule. Like ionic particles sharing electrons, these people circled around hundreds of others who whirled around hundreds of others who spun around hundreds of others, ad infinitum. None of them knew how many lives they touched in such a nebulous way. Some people would never know it could ever be important. But then, *some* people would *never* pay attention.

At the moment, Tony was concerned that a particularly attractive soul in front of him wasn't paying attention. Such *eyes*, he thought. The young man in question had been distracted by a commotion that had begun somewhere outside the pool gate and was growing in volume like an approaching invasion of crazed parrots.

Like an explosion, an oddly dressed assortment of people burst through the gate, careening around the patio. Each of them had on a sort of pseudo-military outfit, but sewn with satin and sequins and epaulets adorned with peacock feathers; and each wore ballet slippers. Those who weren't shooting stopper arrows at the guests were flinging showers of gold and silver glitter dust in the air like a squadron of godmothers.

"Bibbity, boppity," they screamed, lurching around in an attempt at dance.

Under each satin army jacket, they all wore lavender T-shirts, sprinkled with glittered hearts and the words "Heart Attack" across each chest or breast.

The captain of this crew, distinguished by a Napoleonic hat, a long feather boa, serious knee length riding boots and a matching leather crop, strutted around with one hand in his vest, paging Elizabeth.

"Dr. McKay . . . Dr. Elizabeth McKay," he entoned through a well-developed set of upper crust adenoids.

Amid the chaos, Elizabeth lay on a deck chair, laughing at Kincaid's elaborate efforts to entertain her. And surely Tony had had a hand in it.

Stopper arrows were flying everywhere as the rest of the party pressed around Elizabeth, hooting and chuckling and ducking.

Tony snatched up a spent arrow, licked the end and planted it on his forehead. Then he swooned into the arms of the beboaed captain. "Oh, beat me, beat me. Make me write bad checks," Tony moaned, doing his best Camille.

"Dr. McKay!" screamed the captain. "Medic, medic!"

Elizabeth raised on one elbow and waved with the other hand. "Over here, Captain. I surrender."

The Heart Attack squadron scurried around in premeditated indecision, bouncing off each other like inflated Keystone Kops, and finally arranged themselves into a stopperded arch that fanned away from Elizabeth's feet.

"Pres-e-e-ent . . . kazoo!" bellowed the captain. Ten kazoos flew to twenty lips, and amid a fuzzy fanfare, Kincaid appeared carrying a huge cake. In the center of it, in a flash of colored icing, a familiar polo player sat astride a large green alligator.

"Who are you trying to kid, Kincaid?" Tony said, punching her in the ribs. "You didn't bake that thing. The only icing you know about was in last winter's weather report."

"Tell *me*, Grace." Kincaid said. "This is no B-Team brunch. This is your basic designer cake in basic designer chocolate. Napkins by Halston."

Laughter rippled through the crowd. Hardly anyone had been spared Kincaid's diatribe on the Designer Syndrome. She felt, and often said that dressing well is one thing, but this designer hooha was just the middle class equivalent of Minnie Pearl's hat. Kincaid still bought the stuff, but she cut the labels off. She hated labels, especially expensive ones. Elizabeth just smiled indulgently when she caught her snipping away at a new sweater, and gave her a soothing, half-teasing hug. Then she would reach in Kincaid's hope chest and pull out something left to Kincaid by her grandmother and wrap it around Kincaid's shoulders. She called it Kincaid's bleeding heart, liberal, upper class quilt.

Elizabeth loved the effort Kincaid went to in order to please her, and she laughed along with everyone else as Kincaid knelt slowly beside her, placing the cake on a low table.

She took two glasses of champagne from Tony, handed one to Elizabeth and raised her glass. But there was no toast necessary; Elizabeth could see all she ever needed to know shining in Kincaid's eyes. And heard it in the feel of those gentle, slow lips on her own before Kincaid leaned away from her an inch and said softly, as if no one else were there, "Who's my favorite, Angel?"

Elizabeth closed her eyes with the feel of that voice that bore to the center of her. Always. Still. And she drew the day all close around her, the people she loved and who loved her, like a warm shawl of sunlight. Then she looked at those most special eyes and answered this question that had become ritual between them, this vow between two lovers.

"Me," Elizabeth breathed and cupped Kincaid's face gently in one hand.

* * *

Elizabeth's party officially had started an hour before noon with enough food to choke a herd, so although it was barely after sundown, even the hard core bunch had gone home. Some were still hungry though. Not for food or drink, but for more of the electricity that this crowd always generated. The likely place this energy was expected to be found was among allegedly similar people, and that meant The Bar. There were lots of Gay bars in town, but going to any of them was simply Going To The Bar. A coded phrase left over no doubt from the days when there *was* only one.

There were a dozen bars by the time Elizabeth met Kincaid, although they didn't meet in one of them. Elizabeth and Tony had gone to the symphony and at intermission, as she stood in one of the lines leading to the wines and champagne, she looked toward the adjacent line and almost moaned aloud. The woman who was causing her this fit of the vapors wore an elegantly sensuous black gown over slender, bronzed flesh. Kincaid was talking to someone in front of her but for some reason, she stopped in mid-sentence, turned her head and looked directly into Elizabeth's eyes with what Elizabeth remembered as undisguised lust. Kincaid's eyes pierced Elizabeth's, left them, traveled slowly down the length of Elizabeth's legs, up them again and back into her eyes. Then Kincaid turned to the bartender and ordered two glasses of wine as Elizabeth fought to regain consciousness. The next thing Elizabeth knew, Kincaid was at her side offering her one of the glasses she held and steering her into a corner away from the crowd and finding out the better part of her life story by the time Beethoven came between them. They met for dinner the next night and from then on it would have been pushing the river with a sieve for them to stop.

Like everybody else, Elizabeth knew the code words, the places to mention, the books and authors to name in order to identify other "members of the church," as she put it, so it didn't take long to establish that neither of them had to be converted.

Elizabeth had been in love before but for the wrong reasons, or with the wrong person, and she had not been seeing anyone in particular for over a year. Kincaid, who had recently sworn never to live with anyone again, started mentally placing her furniture the first time she walked in the apartment Elizabeth had then had. And Kincaid stopped going to the bar, an event which, to those who knew her, presaged the millenium.

Kincaid still wasn't interested in going to the bar; tonight she had other things on her mind and they only included Elizabeth. But she knew they both needed to talk to Tony and David, so she asked them to stay after everyone else left. From the kitchen, she could hear Elizabeth well into an adequate mad.

"I don't know what they're up to," Elizabeth growled. "But I'm damn well going to find out! Chuck told me *Fred* gave my notes to him. How the hell did *Fred* get them? And why?"

"Well," Tony sighed, still thinking about the new young man who had left without him. Thwarted, he thought. Do you get that way from playing with frogs or princes? An image of Chuck's angular features surfaced in his head and he sighed. Handsome, yes; but there was something about Chuck that Tony didn't trust, and he'd already had several tangles with him. Chuck was forever injecting himself into Tony's office business whether an inoculation was requested or not. Chuck had an arrogant way about him and an annoying habit of referring to Tony as "my man" and "old man." Still, he was undeniably handsome if all else could be ignored. "Chuck may be an arrogant sonofabitch, but he sure—" he paused slightly, his eyes mischievous. Elizabeth and David both knew what was coming.

"—sure is hunky," they chanted in unison with him.

He looked sheepishly from one to the other of them. "I know," he pouted. "Keep my hands in my pockets." They didn't look as if they believed him. "Oh, come *on*. I'm not into straight men. No offense, David."

David bowed lightly, indicating that none was taken. Kincaid and Kathy had been picking at the party mess half-heartedly and finally joined the others in the breakfast room. Kathy kissed her husband on the neck and refilled his wine glass, passing the empty bottle to Kincaid, who went to the kitchen in search of a replacement.

Kincaid and Elizabeth had an understanding about shared responsibility regarding the house: Elizabeth messed it up; Kincaid picked it up. And they both got outsiders to help when they couldn't manage their division of labor alone.

"I checked with a friend in Personnel yesterday," said David. "The bottom line, Elizabeth, in that you're our best chance with Curtis. Women have specific laws about equal pay, even if they aren't enforced. Being Jewish and underpaid doesn't count."

"And I ain't *tellin'*," said Tony, "what minority *I* belong to."

"No, shit, Sherlock," Elizabeth said, tweaking Tony's cheek lovingly. "Best cover I ever had."

Kincaid returned from the kitchen with a new bottle of wine and looked at Kathy. "She told me *I* was the best lover she ever had."

"*Cover*, lambchops, with a *C*," Elizabeth smiled at her.

"Good lord," Kincaid chided. "*Covers*. You two kill me. Don't you think people might get just a little suspicious when we're all sixty? You two are still *dating*, and I'm still your *roommate*?"

Kincaid's opinion of the efficiency of "covers" was that they weren't in the least. To her, Gay relationships were perfectly obvious to anyone with brains enough to whistle Dixie. She conceded that most people didn't have occasion to demonstrate their intelligence in this manner or the occasion to think about anything they assumed to be alien. If forced to think, people believed what suited their own purposes. These people, for Kincaid, fell into three categories: those who knew but preferred the comfortable, rosy illusion of ignorance; those who knew and were either pleased or unaffected; and those who knew and wanted your hide either on a barn door or in their own beds. Kincaid's headings for these categories were: A.) parents, B.) friends and C.) evangelists, religious or otherwise.

Looking at Tony, Elizabeth pointed at Kincaid behind her hand. "Your basic designer radical Lesbian feminist. If it weren't for me keeping her on a short political leash, she'd be out marching in the streets."

Presented now with the lofty view from her favorite soap box, Kincaid could see their world clearly yet again. "The closet is an oppressive, self-perpetuating little box. The greatest idea I ever heard was the one about waking up lavender."

Kathy looked confused. "Waking up who?"

"Lavender, love," said Tony, "as in the color of the Gay national banner."

"Oh," said Kathy, no closer to clarity than before.

Kincaid loved to be in charge of providing clarity on any and all occasions. "Since it's so hard to figure out who's Gay and who's not, and how much of what behavior equals one certified *homosexual*," she said the word sounding like Vincent Price, flashing a ghoulish face and wiggling taloned fingers at Kathy, "it would help if everyone could be color-coded. People who have only *thought* about committing *The Act* would get one small lavender dot in the center of his or her forehead."

"A pale one," Tony said in his Eleanor Roosevelt voice.

Kincaid ignored Eleanor. "Reading about it with above average interest might rate two dots. For each actual experience, you could have larger, darker spots. *Heterosexual* experiences," she said this like Vincent again, just as ominously, and pointed to David and Kathy, "known by some as the Dire Straights," she paused as everyone groaned, "could get pink and scarlet splotches."

Eleanor rolled his eyes and hiked his voice up another notch. "Oh, how *tasteful*!"

David looked from Tony to Kincaid and pronounced pointedly, "*Some* of us wouldn't have sufficient surface area for that much color coding."

Kincaid cast languid vamp eyes at Elizabeth. "Lust means always having to say you're sorry."

Tony nodded, wisdom of the ages herself, and said to David, "And what *hue* would you wake up, Miss Thing?"

"Jewish," David said dryly.

"Bluish?!" Kathy was aghast.

"Jesus," Elizabeth exhaled before David could repeat himself, so he mouthed the word to Kathy again, and she looked relieved. "Can't anyone *hear* at this table? Could we get on with some business some time within the next decade?"

"You know we're with you on this, Elizabeth," David said. "But I still think you'll have to sue. They never fix these things without a fight. Even if Curtis wanted to adjust our salaries, which he doesn't, they'd find some way to avoid it or stall it. Or lose the memo on it."

Kathy looked at her husband, "You always make it sound like the place is full of incompetence."

"It isn't incompetence," Tony said, shaking his head. "It's the system. You can't blame it on individuals. There aren't any. The system doesn't allow individuals."

"Bull puckey!" Kincaid leapt into the conversation. "That attitude is what *makes* systems not work. Individuals act. Individuals can take responsibility."

Tony touched a finger to his tongue and reached out to Kincaid's bare arm, tentatively dotting it with his moist tip. He jerked it away as though testing a hot iron and let out a hiss between his teeth.

Snorting at him, she laughed and grabbed his neck in a half-Nelson, tickling him as he squirmed. Tickling could reduce even the strongest man to jelly, as she well knew.

"Girls are so rough," Tony gasped to David. "When boys fight, we just break each other's china and crystal."

From the patio, they could still hear party music being pumped out by the stereo. There was a small pause and a woman's voice broke into "What I Did for Love."

Tony sprang to his feet and grabbed Elizabeth. "Get up, girls!" he shouted, "It's the national anthem!"

"We're *women*, Tony," Kincaid almost huffed, more seriously than she sounded. "If *your* consciousness hasn't been raised, who's *can* be?"

Tony looked momentarily despondent. "Let's not discuss my *raising* anything tonight, dear. Doing that alone is said to cause ophthalmic deficiencies."

When Elizabeth finally got them back to the topic at hand (and she defied Tony to comment further on her choice of words), it seemed there was no progress to be made until after she heard from Curtis. Kincaid reminded them, Elizabeth in particular, that planning the war one battle at a time was short sighted. She was of the Big Stick School for Diplomacy which held that one should know the contents of one's arsenal, the size of the biggest muzzle and the last straw on which it rested. Before the first shot. They yawned, ignored her and went home to await Monday.

Thirty seconds after Tony left, always the last one out, their doorbell rang again. It usually took two trips for Tony to collect everything he came with, so Elizabeth wasn't surprised until she opened the door.

"Lisa!" Elizabeth stopped and looked at the shyness on Lisa's face. "Is something wrong?"

Lisa hesitated. Maybe she shouldn't have come. "No . . . I . . . just wanted to see you. To apologize for skipping yesterday's session." Her eyes found Elizabeth's and she swallowed hard. "I hope it's not . . . that is . . . can I come in?"

"Oh. Sure. Of course," Elizabeth smiled. Nothing's wrong? But why's she here? "How'd you know how to find the house?"

"I convinced your secretary I needed to see you, to show you something. My excuse for Friday." Lisa smiled, feeling a little less nervous, and as she looked around, she saw wrapping paper and ribbons strewn around the living room. "Looks like a party just died," she said.

"My birthday. There's still cake left. Want some?"

"Sure . . . yeah. That'd be nice. Can I ask which birthday or is that against the rules?"

"My rules don't include that one. I'm thirty-three."

Lisa's mouth rounded in surprise. She hadn't really thought of Elizabeth as much older than herself, as if she were only a year or so ahead of her in school. "You sure don't look that old. That is, well." She stopped, embarrassing herself. "That's not old exactly. I mean. . . ."

Elizabeth laughed and touched Lisa's shoulder. "I know. At twenty-one, everybody else is either terminally naive or coasting toward senility. I felt the same way. Thought that surely by twenty-eight I'd need a cane. If I lasted that long. But I guess the Lord still has something in mind for me to do."

They heard the back door close, and Kincaid stuck her head around the kitchen door. "Coffee's ready." Kincaid had expected Tony to be standing there and was surprised when she saw Lisa, but her smile was automatic. Pretty faces always made her smile. "Oh, hi," Kincaid said. What was it she saw in this young woman's eyes? Disappointment? How could I have disappointed the girl, Kincaid thought. I haven't had time.

"Kincaid, this is Lisa Hunter," Elizabeth said quickly, her eyes flashing a silent caution. "Lisa, Kincaid Phillips. Lisa is a student at the University."

Lisa extended her hand and smiled. She realized though that for some reason she was disconcerted. She had expected, even hoped that Elizabeth would be alone. But surely that wasn't it. Maybe it was because Kincaid was, well, stunning. That was the word. She had felt stunned by the woman, as if she'd turned the corner and run into a film star or a model whose face she'd seen a thousand times but didn't really believe it existed without an air brush and soft focus lens. Now she knew where she'd seen that face before. It was next to Dr. McKay's in a photograph in her office. And now she recognized her feeling. Whenever she saw that photograph of the two of them together, arms around each other, she felt something like jealousy, though surely that wasn't it. She didn't want to think about that feeling, so she clowned her way ahead of its pursuing little feet. She had learned without being taught that she should hide her feelings if they caught up with her. From Jake she had learned that a clown's mask is intended to hide something.

"Actually," she said in an amplified stage whisper to Kincaid, "I'm one of her crazies."

"Only if you think you're going to get a session on my birthday," Elizabeth joked. "Since you don't seem to need one."

"Just coffee, I promise." Lisa's eyes sparkled, and she flashed her smile again. "Oh, wait till you see! Come to the window. My excuse is outside!" She spun on her heel and swung wide around the couch, the wind from her body rustling through the palms. As she arched her hips sideways, Elizabeth heard a dull thud and something that sounded like a barbell being dropped on the floor. Lisa grabbed her hip and groaned in pain.

"Oh, God. The iron dog, Elizabeth!" Kincaid trotted into the kitchen in search of first aid.

"Oh, no," Elizabeth sighed apologetically, reaching toward Lisa. "Are you ok?"

Returning with a plastic bag full of ice, Kincaid pointed toward the cast iron Doberman which Lisa had knocked to the floor. "That thing's got killer instincts, Elizabeth." She smiled sympathetically at Lisa. "Just be glad you aren't taller."

Silently assessing where the statue's nose could have struck had her legs been longer, Lisa grinned as she pressed the bag to her bruise. "I'm ok. But why do you have him hiding here in the bushes?"

"The great cat trainer's idea," Kincaid said, pointing to Elizabeth. "She says it's supposed to intimidate her kitty. To keep the little omnivore from chewing on the plants. She says."

Fingering a few semi-digested fronds, Lisa shook her head. "It's not working too well."

"Hey!" Elizabeth shouted, looking out the window. "You've got a new car. Just like mine. Only cleaner."

"I know. Hot, aren't they?" Lisa hobbled to the window. "Now if I can just drive home with one leg."

"Coffee's hot, gimpette. Come out by the pool," Kincaid said, then pointed to the iron dog. "And watch out for Poindexter."

One pot of coffee didn't last long enough to suit Lisa. She hoped Kincaid would leave before she herself had stayed beyond politeness. But after the second cup, it began not to matter anyway because Kincaid was in rare form. Lisa was enjoying herself more than she had in an age; she couldn't help but like a woman who made her laugh so easily. And whose looks were as arresting as Elizabeth's.

Kincaid had decided to play one of her favorite games: Harass the Cat. Around and around the pool chugged a small wind-up fluffy baby duck that made weird little noises. Amelia stalked it in agitated confusion, propelled by the equal but opposing certitudes of the gourmand and the hydrophobic.

"Kincaid, get that thing out of the pool. She's going to overcome her cowardice one of these days, jump at that duck and drown." It was difficult for Elizabeth to sound concerned while she was laughing.

"You kidding? She hates water so bad she could fall in, touch bottom and be out before she got wet." Kincaid hooted as Amelia almost fell in, but saved herself without grace, her adrenalin stripping her gears into reverse and outjuicing her saliva. "You'd think, after so many demonstrations, she'd realize that the wee beastie cat can*not* walk on water."

As if concurring in Kincaid's observation, Amelia abruptly rose out of stalk position, strolled over to Lisa and hopped in her lap, the duck ignored and thus forgotten. Amelia was a creature of the here and now, which to her justified selective inattention and the resulting gaps in her view of history.

"Is this supposed to be a compliment?" Lisa asked, her stomach just so much biscuit dough to Amelia.

"Only to those who like cats," Kincaid confided as she picked up the empty coffee pot. "Take my advice and keep your distance. Terminal tuna breath. Anybody want more coffee? I'm about wired for sound myself."

Lisa hesitated. "No . . . no, I guess not." Kincaid gathered the cups and went toward the kitchen. "I've stayed too long as it is anyway," she said to Elizabeth.

"Nonsense. I'm glad you came by to show me your excuse. Although it is one of the most expensive ever used on me."

Lisa felt a tightening in her stomach when Elizabeth smiled at her, felt transparent again and so looked away from Elizabeth's eyes.

Amelia, frequently malcontent if not at the dead center of attention, rescued Lisa in the silence and offered her giant economy size ears as something to do with her hands.

"I like your house," Lisa said finally. "It's awfully big for just one person."

"Two. Kincaid lives here, too."

A light went on in a small, distant, little-used room in Lisa's head, a place she avoided and would have disavowed any knowledge of. The only awareness she allowed of the room or the light, before it went out, was the little shadow it threw across her face.

"Cuts expenses, huh?" Lisa said as Amelia bumped and purred and kneaded her way back into the conversation. "Insistent little devil, isn't she? What's her name?"

Elizabeth smiled. "Amelia . . . Amelia *Ear*heart."

Lisa smiled, too, and ran her hand the length of the silky, perfumed fur. As Elizabeth reached to touch her cat, she inadvertently covered Lisa's hand instead, just as Kincaid came out the kitchen door. Both women saw Lisa's body go rigid for an instant. Elizabeth smiled gently, but Lisa could read nothing in it or in her eyes. Probably because Elizabeth wasn't sending any messages other than to relax.

The kitchen screen door banged shut, and Lisa looked at Kincaid, feeling somehow caught, though she didn't know doing what. Suddenly she felt confused and disappointed. She'd had this feeling often, but couldn't remember the context. It was almost like the time, when only a little girl, she had smelled a mango and wanted to taste it. She hadn't known its exotic name, so she'd asked her mother for a flat pear. And, of course, what she'd gotten was not what she wanted. There is, after all, everything in a name.

She put Amelia on the ground and stood nervously. Being confused always made her edgy. "Listen, thanks for the coffee. Even though I am old enough for something stronger. Or strong enough for something older," she clowned. "Whatever."

* * *

Elizabeth watched Lisa walk to her car and waited until she was safely in it with the door locked and the engine on before she closed the front door. When she turned around, Kincaid was staring knowingly at her. Knowing looks irritated Elizabeth, because they implied that the wearer actually possessed unique information about someone else, a property rarely if ever available as far as Elizabeth was concerned.

"What's the intense look for, Anna Freud?" Elizabeth asked, wanting nonetheless to be privy also to whatever this insight might be.

Kincaid touched a finger to her forehead. "Lavender dots. That girl has a crush on you."

"That *woman*," Elizabeth corrected gently and smiled. "And she doesn't. I know you have these nagging suspicions, but every woman is not a potential Gay blade-ette. And all those who currently exist do not have a crush on me."

"Both hypotheses are debatable." Kincaid loved for people to have crushes on Elizabeth. Each one merely confirmed her own good judgment.

She followed Elizabeth into the kitchen, always expecting a miracle, but Elizabeth waved away even tentative thoughts of cleaning up the aftermath. Kincaid resigned herself to tomorrow's fate as maid and consoled herself by wringing out the last of the champagne before following Elizabeth to their bedroom.

"Don't you think it's a little dangerous, though," she persisted. "I mean if she is Gay? To be her therapist."

"You sound like that full time professional insufferable twit at work. It's not dangerous. Just . . . difficult. Besides, it's not up to me to decide who Lisa is. It's up to Lisa. And she hasn't done that yet. What's dangerous, Pope Etta, is name-calling. No matter who does it."

Kincaid drew herself up in exaggerated haughtiness. "Weh-eh-ehll. Miss *Thing*." Then she stuck her hands in Elizabeth's face and wiggled her fingers to match the witch face she was making. "Oh, booga, booga. Come down off that pulpit before you get a nose bleed."

"My pulpit's no higher than your soapbox. Besides. Black pots don't get nose bleeds. Only kettles do." She stuck out her tongue and turned toward her closet to undress.

Kincaid knew it was time to change the subject, and she just happened to have her favorite one handy. With a smoldering look always only a breath away from flaming, she reached out and touched Elizabeth's shoulder. Is it telepathy, Elizabeth thought, that she knows me so well? Or do we just have the same rhythm, hear the same music.

"Last tag," Kincaid breathed, her hand sliding under Elizabeth's hair to her neck, her eyes flashing with what had become a ritual invitation, and it made Elizabeth melt as if it were again the first time.

The first time. World without end. Amen. Amen.

* * *

Kincaid woke before Elizabeth and gently disentangled herself from the leggy web they had woven around each other the night before. It was still amazing to her they got any sleep at all. During their first year, Kincaid thought she'd have to take a room at the Ramada, alone, just to get her wind back.

Fortunately they had still not, after five years together, come to their senses. She thought people who came to their senses were insane.

She had come to this relationship by a rather circuitous route. At least she had thought it circuitous, until she had compared stories with a few people and found her history, of all tedious things, common.

In retrospect, of course, Kincaid could see that women had always played the most significant roles in her life. That she had been attracted to a number of them, especially during and after prep school, seemed perfectly normal to her. All the girls drooled over models and movie stars and each other, the same way they drooled over their boyfriends.

She began to suspect that she might be different when she couldn't work up the same degree of enthusiasm when the models were in Marlboro ads and the movie was *A Fist Full of Dollars*. But she continued to like the "each other" part. Intuitively, she knew not to act on these attractions or to discuss them, having read and wanting to believe the seemingly holy and therefore immortal myth of A Phase She Was Going Through.

In order to goose herself toward a terminal rigor of what seemed her interminable phase, she dated men feverishly like it was going out of style and finally got married, at her parent's insistence, just after law school. To a sweet man that she loved. At the time, she didn't know the monumental contribution two prepositions could make to a word. Love is wonderful all by its lonesome, but *in* and *with* make heaven.

In college, she could remember sorority sisters lamenting the most recent poor behavior on the part of their most recent boyfriend, concluding with a disdainful, "Men! But what's the *alternative*?" Had she known there was one, she felt that maybe she could have spared herself and her husband the hurt and confusion that came with her discovery of those prepositions. In secret. With a woman.

She still loved her ex-husband, though not the way he wanted, and she didn't know how to tell him why without hurting him even more than she had already. She was afraid to tell him when they were first divorced because she knew he would tell the people at the club, and she liked the facilities there, the sauna and steam room which had given a whole new meaning to the word "facilities" since it was here she had so easily found her first woman lover. She eventually convinced herself that her ex-husband knew anyway. If he wanted to talk about it, he could bring it up himself. She'd been living with Elizabeth five years. How could he *not* know?

Actually, he had brought it up once, years ago. He and she had been having one of their infrequent lunches when a woman she knew from the bar had stopped and spoken familiarly to her. The woman was a severe person who made no effort to soften anything about herself, not her walk nor her voice, and she rarely smiled. When this sergeant major of a woman finally stumped away, he stared at Kincaid, then back at the woman and down at his avocado. Finally he said, "That new friend of yours. Is she Gay?"

Kincaid lost her balance only momentarily. "I don't think she's even potentially frivolous," she laughed unconvincingly.

But that had been during her first affair when she had been just beginning to admit that she found more women attractive than just her current lover. That was the second step toward naming herself out loud.

When she "came out," as they say, the doors to the closet were left dangling on demolished hinges. It took less than a year for her to make her way from her original four-by-four closet to the two-and-half bath frame of mind which she had now occupied for some years. But she was beginning to feel the paralysis of cramped quarters again. Not for another lover; she couldn't imagine herself without Elizabeth. But she wanted more freedom to be honest and open about herself.

It never failed to amaze her that women could be stuck for years, decades even, in the four-by-four self-definition that, "I'm in love with a person (*One after another?*) who *happens* to be a woman. But *I'm* not Gay!"

But then she'd stop herself in her tirade against the chicken livers of the world and remember Elizabeth, who wanted to believe that who you love is really nobody's business. That selecting your own name ultimately is something done alone, a process that ends only in death, she said, if then.

No doubt that was also when Kincaid would stop preaching about the political significance of coming out. If then.

Elizabeth thought it significant and amusing that Kincaid, for all her Come-out-come-out-wherever-you-are insistence, religiously avoided even *saying* the word *Lesbian*. She used Gay because, she said, she had *chosen* to. She didn't care what radical separatists said about the political significance of being identified as the women of Gay men, she had never liked the word. "I'm not *from* the Isle of Lesbos. I was *born* in *Boston*," Kincaid would blast as she stomped off in a huff.

"The defense rests," Elizabeth would respond quietly to Kincaid's everlasting mortification.

The defense is just beginning, thought Kincaid, supposing she was on another case entirely, as she hustled around the kitchen requiring mortal eggs and cheese to rise to the occasion they were about to attend. Known locally as A Little Something for Elizabeth.

She arranged the breakfast trays just so, complete with roses and fresh breads, and headed toward the bedroom with her creations.

Amelia had already decided it was time for her massage and was doing her best to rouse the masseuse, who remained stubbornly intent on her decadence.

Moving like an acrobat, Kincaid swooped in and set both trays on the bed gingerly, then bounded out the door, full of energy. "If either of you two knock over those culinary delights," she called over her shoulder, "I'll shove you in the trash compactor."

Opening one eye, Elizabeth surveyed the abundant contents of the bed, yawned, and began engineering herself into a less than prone position under her tray. Amelia leapt from the bed, streaking for the kitchen, where she knew Kincaid had left a similar sampling for her. It had originally been not Elizabeth's, but Kincaid's and Amelia's discriminating palates that had prompted these excesses.

Kincaid came back to the bed with an ice bucket and champagne and slid carefully back into her nest beside her lover.

"What's the occasion?" Elizabeth yawned.

"The day after your birthday and the day before your personal independence day." Kincaid filled the glasses and passed one over. Elizabeth, still seeing the world through cobwebs of sleep, took the glass and looked at Kincaid like an alien.

"D-Day. VJ-Day. Ten Sixty-six," explained Kincaid, garbling around a mouthful of heaven. "Tomorrow is Monday. We have met the enemy and he is Fred."

Elizabeth melted back down into the covers with an enormous sigh bubbling redundantly into her champagne. "And I was having such an incredibly wonderful Freudian dream."

"Freudian dreams aren't wonderful. They're sexist. Here, drink your coffee and talk to me like a reasonably alert humanoid. Time to map out your strategy for tomorrow."

"At this hour? How can you even move after last night? Much less think?"

"Don't get me off the subject. What time do you meet with the dilbert?"

"Four-thirty." Elizabeth began to see virtue in the tray before her and threw an unusual wad of something to the beast in her innards.

"And you will do what?"

"Demand just and swift recompense."

"Or?"

"His first born male child."

"No. I think the law suit comes next. Then the child."

"Oh."

Kincaid munched on three or four other things while she thought. "Dr. Chuckington Gardner sounds like a real asshole."

"No, actually an asshole performs a *useful* bodily function."

"Well, just remember: There are two purposes in life. Chuck's must be to serve as the *bad* example." Kincaid twisted a strand of her dark hair and looked at Elizabeth. "So, what are you going to say to Curtis about those notes on Lisa?"

Elizabeth's eyes sprang open, then narrowed again, nailing her coffee cup as if it were Curtis. "That's the *first* thing on the agenda!"

"Atta girl!" Kincaid jumped into her old cheerleader routine. "*Have* a little righteous indignation with that champagne! *Stand* up for those principles, girl!"

"Damn right!"

"Tomorrow's the deadline, then? You're committed?"

"I may have to *be* committed if this thing doesn't go well." Her voice lost a little of its resolve. "Why do people always insist on being forced to be fair? Confrontation is just not my style."

"The hell it isn't! You may not like to fight, but you can't stand to lose. Especially to someone not worth the effort."

"*That's* true." She banged her coffee cup into its saucer for punctuation. "It just takes so much time and energy. My job takes almost more than I've got." She sighed tiredly. "What a dumb futhermucker. What a waste of everybody's time."

Kincaid set down her champagne and turned toward her, tracing Elizabeth's fine, precise jaw and cheek, half-hidden by that mane of soft auburn hair.

"Nothing, Sweet-Precious . . . *nothing* is *ever* a waste."

She extended her hand toward Elizabeth, in a half-fist, palm up with the first two fingers pointing together. "Gimme two," she said gruffly, imitating the sound of what she imagined would come from a run-of-the-mill macho throat.

Elizabeth looked at her for a long moment, smiled and popped Kincaid's fingers with two of her own. Another ritual: this parody of an athlete's victory greeting. A symbol of connection. And commitment.

Elizabeth set both full trays on the floor, her eyes smoldering. Breakfast would have to wait. Again.

* * *

PART V

"*You did what*?" Curtis roared like a tuba in heat. His jowls ballooned out and glowed red and purple like a pomegranate, his lips pursed and fluted around a toothpick stem.

"It was an *accident*, Fred!" Chuck pleaded, backing across Curtis' office and holding up both palms toward Curtis as if to shield himself from the fire in the pudgy man's eyes.

"*I* didn't give you those notes! What the hell would *I* be doing with them? Jesus God in almighty heaven!" If he hadn't been in his office, he would have spit, toothpick and all. He might anyway. "Why in blazing Hades didn't you *call* me this *weekend*?" The fact that his rowboat was not equipped with telephone escaped his attention; Chuck couldn't have gotten in touch with him had he attempted to because Curtis never told his wife where he did his fishing and thus prevented her from reaching him with the kind of tidings he had just received. He looked around for something to spit in and almost settled on Chuck's face. "Around here, son, lying is grounds for immediate dismissal," he threatened, his eyes pinched into slits.

"I didn't have any choice, Fred! Listen to me. It was the only way out for both of us. She caught me coming out of your office with her notes in my hand. Look. The explanation will work."

Curtis calmed not a whit down, but he was listening.

"Look, you had every reason to need those notes. If you suspected Elizabeth of sleeping with a student . . . a *patient* . . . a *girl* . . .! If she'd been accused of it, you'd have to check it out. And you'd have to get an expert's opinion about the—"

"Thanks to you, I don't have any options about using that shit!" Fred hissed.

"What other options are there?"

Curtis cut his eyes at Chuck and stared icily at him. Options had never been his long suit.

* * *

Outside on the practice field, scarred helmets glinted in the late afternoon light. Jake took the snap from center and backpeddled, looking toward the sidelines for Scooter. The school's best and his favorite wide receiver was charging hard toward the goal line. But not hard enough. Jake fired the ball in Scooter's direction and was simultaneously slammed in the ribs by two hurtling, hulking linemen, sandwiched to the turf like a slab of ham. The ball sailed in a perfect spiral toward Scooter's desperate fingertips and on beyond them, landing in the end zone unescorted and spent. On the sidelines, Coach Crutcher clutched his whistle in his fist and rifled it into the grass. His won-lost scale had been plunging dangerously to the right, threatening to spill his career and his future, a future that always rested on younger shoulders.

Curtis stood in his office, watching, yet not seeing, the scrimmage outside his window. He rocked forward on the balls of his feet, slapping his fist into the palm of his other hand in broken rhythm with his rocking. He stopped, his gaze out of focus, looking somewhere toward mythology. Seeing nothing but haze, he discarded that wisp of an idea and began rocking and slapping again; as if by this physical thought process, he could forge some workable, tangible decision with his fist instead of his brain.

The buzz of his intercom ranted into his consciousness, and he started like a rabbit. Striding impatiently to his desk, he punched the nagging box.

"What is it, Martha? I told you to hold my calls. I'm very busy."

At her desk, Martha closed her eyes and paused for a moment of prayer, asking for assistance, patience, the flu, or some dead white man's birthday to show up soon on the calendar. She flicked her box to transmit. "It's four-twenty-five, Fred. You said to remind you. Elizabeth's waiting."

Curtis looked at his watch. "OK, Martha," he exhaled. "Tell her to step in here in about, oh, ten minutes."

On the corner of his desk sat the Rubik's cube Chuck had solved and with which Curtis had promptly and irreparably fiddled. He picked it up absently and moved to the window, turning the sections of the puzzle in randomly deliberate confusion. Sweat on his upper lip sparkled like tiny helmets.

He stopped twisting the sections and smacked the cube into his thinking palm, held it a moment, then slammed it down on the sill, splintering the puzzle piece that would eventually have led him through the riddle. Had he known where to start. Or cared about such elusive things as solutions.

"Shit!" he exploded. And he launched a wad of spittle toward his wilting, yellowing philodendron, who was grateful at this point for any attention at all.

Down the hall, Elizabeth played the caged tigress in front of Martha's desk. The outer office was empty as was usual in the afternoon. Students didn't like afternoon appointments, and committees for some reason did. Since every committee had to have a female administrator on it, that species being so hard to locate on campus, Elizabeth had more than her share of afternoon commitments. She had cancelled two to meet with Curtis.

"Think he's ready for me yet, Martha?"

"The truth? He'll *never* be ready for you."

Elizabeth smiled a small one.

"If he gives you any trouble," Martha conspired, her black eyes mischievous, "you let me know. I'll send out his memos the way he writes them. That'll fix his happy hieney." She looked at her watch, then at Elizabeth and pointed toward Curtis' door. "You don't need it, but good luck anyway."

Elizabeth touched her arm affectionately. Martha knew absolutely everything that was going on in the office except what was said in private counseling sessions. Everything else was covered and verified and documented in memo after memo, in triplicate and "quadraplegic," as Fred said, more accurately than he knew. So she knew precisely what the meeting was about and its almost foregone conclusion: Fred was dead wrong, had finally done something so blatantly in error that he'd have to back down, and was just minutes away from a long overdue comeuppance.

Her smile glistened at Elizabeth's back as it disappeared into Curtis' office.

Inside, Curtis was seated in his swivel chair, wailing and moaning its rusty springs as he swung around to see Elizabeth. He wiped his face, from his upper lip down, dredged up the least authentic smile Elizabeth had ever seen him forge, and swung his feet up on his desk clumsily, hitting something small and round.

There was the indicative electronic click from Martha's intercom and she waited for whatever order was about to ensue.

What she heard, simultaneously from down the hall into one ear and out of the unit into her other, was Curtis' paternal voice.

"Come on in, Lizbuth," he dueted with himself. "Close the door so we can have some privacy."

For an instant, Martha considered getting up and telling Curtis to turn off his intercom. He hit the fool thing with his feet at least twice a day, and she always had to get up and go tell him. Why he didn't get a newer unit was no mystery to her. This one was not an inconvenience to *him*.

It still amazed her how people could do something over and over and still be surprised by the result. Like, for instance: crushed ice in the bottom of a glass, with one sip of cola left. She had never seen it fail. Sit there draining that last sweet drop slowly away from the ice, and watching those chips, knowing what's bound to happen. But soon as the ice falls all over their face, what do they do? Jump. Like it'd never happened to them before, and they'd never heard of gravity.

Martha, praying that Elizabeth would be either the ice or the gravity, leaned a little closer to her intercom and turned up the volume. Through the speaker and down the hall, she heard the door close.

* * *

Kincaid lay on the couch in the living room re-reading the gospel according to Kate Millett. Her copy of *Sexual Politics* that she held in one hand had been dogeared and underlined and exclaimed and starred until it had gained a pound of ink since its printing. Kincaid had come to feminism slightly tardy, but the more she read, the madder she got. And like most new converts she was an evangelist.

She took a sip of wine and drew another exclamation point in the margin as she heard the door open. Elizabeth closed it slowly and leaned her forehead exhaustedly against the dark wood.

Kincaid closed her book and smiled a greeting. Then she saw Elizabeth's dejection and emptiness slumping in her eyes. Kincaid sat up cross-legged as Elizabeth sank into the couch and covered her face with her hands, rubbing her forehead methodically.

"I guess I don't get to break open the champagne, huh," Kincaid said softly.

Elizabeth only dropped her head further, her shoulders deflating in a long sigh.

"I'll draw up the papers tonight, Elizabeth," she said firmly. "Tomorrow we sue."

Elizabeth's voice was tiny, a kitten whispering. "We can't." She looked over her fingertips at Kincaid and a tear slid over her hand.

Kincaid scooted closer to her and smoothed Elizabeth's hair gently. "What do you mean, we can't?" Her voice was puzzled and concerned.

Elizabeth's breath came in little gasps as if her head were being pushed repeatedly under water, her words coming between gasps as if the words were the water. "He said . . . he . . . had been hearing . . . stories about me . . . accusations . . . about me and *Lisa* . . ."

Her voice was full of incredulousness. Then she looked gently at Kincaid. "About me and you." Then, in fear and anger, "He said he was under pressure . . . to *fire* me . . . said those notes, my notes on Lisa were . . ."

"Jesus." Kincaid meant it literally as a prayer, and she closed her eyes under the weight of it and she bowed her head. She put both arms around her lover and drew her close, rocking her slowly like a child. "Angel, Angel. What did you say?"

Elizabeth shook her head weakly. "Denied everything. But my voice shook so, I couldn't have been very convincing, I just never thought. . . ." A broken, choked sob escaped her throat and finished the sentence. Helplessly, Kincaid stroked her lover's neck as if gently trying to heal a wound too critical for medicine, or perhaps even magic.

"I didn't think people at school even thought about us," Elizabeth said disbelievingly, and then her hurt moved sideways to anger. "I certainly don't think about *his* sex life. He does *ducks* for all I care." She wiped her eyes and her anger shown through hot tears. "But when he said those *ridiculous* things about *Lisa* and me—" From deep in her throat came an animal sound; a fierceness clawed at her lungs, a sound Kincaid had never heard but had suspected. "What *right* does he think he has to involve an innocent—"

"Who else has he talked to?" Kincaid interrupted.

Elizabeth dropped loose from the claws of her fury into exhaustion and closed her eyes. "I don't know. Chuck. . . ."

Trying to sound comforting, Kincaid held Elizabeth by her shoulders and looked in her eyes. But she was furious now, too; and she couldn't keep the sound of it inside either. "You haven't done anything to Lisa but help her. Your notes couldn't prove anything."

"They don't have to. Implication is as good as truth to him."

Then Kincaid knew exactly what had happened, why it happened. Her jaw tightened in a rueful clinch, but she held Elizabeth softly. "So you're lucky to have a job at all. And forget about the equal pay."

"Exactly."

Eyes narrowing, Kincaid ground out her words. "That bastard! That's *blackmail!*"

"Bingo." Elizabeth wiped her eyes. "And all the while trying to act so *magnanimous* about it all. Like he was *giving* me something. The last bastion of civil liberties saving me from the witch hunters. Then the threat."

"As long as you don't push for the money."

Elizabeth rubbed her hand across her forehead slowly, as if trying to erase the afternoon's events from her mind.

Exploding off the couch, Kincaid stalked to the mantel and glared at herself in the huge mirror that created another room beyond the fireplace.

"DAMN! Damn! Damn!" she smashed her fist against the mantel. She spun around, the defense not resting at all, her eyes flashing. "Elizabeth, we *can't* let him do this. This is *not* Salem. We are *not* criminals." She softened fiercely. "I love you, Angel. And by *God*, I will not let *anyone* do this to you. To *us*. *He's* broken the law! Not once, but twice!"

"But there's nothing we—"

"We're going to sue that sanctimonious sonofabitch! He's going to wish this was just a class action suit. I seem to recall that blackmail *is* considered criminal. No matter *what* state you're in."

"I can't prove anything Kincaid. Nobody heard him make those threats but me."

"Shit." Kincaid's eyes struck off on another detour and found a path. "You could have recorded it."

"But I didn't."

"*He* doesn't know that."

"Come on, Kincaid. Who's got the law degree here? We can't do that. Anyway, it doesn't matter. Even if we could prove it, and it would stand up in court, what you're talking about is coming *out* out. *Both* of us."

For some reason, Kincaid hadn't considered this a concrete personal possibility. The concepts were still tumbling in the mixer and hadn't been poured yet, let alone had time to set. She didn't have parents or siblings whose feelings had to be sheltered, or worry about an income being cut off; she didn't know the neighbors or care much what they thought. But her ex-husband still didn't know. And somewhere deep in her gut, a noose tightened on something vital and her breath caught. Then she looked at Elizabeth's sad puppy eyes, and she knew what her lover had been feeling, had always felt, because Elizabeth had everybody to explain herself to, everybody to make understand. And how could they do it in a paragraph or a page or a book when it had taken the two of them decades to understand? And reams and reams of worry and delving through thousands of years of lies and isolation and murders and silence, to finally, finally find anger and pride and courage and joy.

But to explain it all, over and over, to people who didn't want to hear. Kincaid felt the exhaustion of redundance before it had even begun. It's not fair, she pleaded silently in her head.

"It's not fair." Elizabeth's whisper echoed aloud, sounding lost, very far away. Kincaid walked to her, cupped her face in her hands and brought her into her arms, stroking her hair and rocking gently, as Elizabeth began to cry softly again.

* * *

"Oh, *shit*, Elizabeth! Did he say anything about *me*?" Tony sat across from Elizabeth in her office and clutched at his stomach as if a small ferocious animal were trying to escape. David cut his silent, reprimanding eyes at him, but waited.

"He isn't after you, Tony. I'm the one bucking the system." Elizabeth's voice was gentle, understanding. She loved Tony better than any man on earth and had no desire to spread the anguish around. Tony looked only a hair relieved.

"Good lord, Tony." David was exasperated. He could afford exasperation, being straight as the ones in Hormuz. "There's more at stake here than your macho image."

"Yeah. *Her* macho image."

"Thanks a lot." Elizabeth said, but she smiled at Tony in spite of herself. Tony's gallows humor had gotten them through a lot. Tony reached across and squeezed her arm, and she could see the sincerity and concern in his eyes. She knew he'd do anything, anything at all to help.

David looked at them, both so seemingly immobilized. "How can you two just sit there?" He stopped in frustration, then plunged on. "It's not the *money* now. You can't let him get away with blackmail!"

"And what is it we're supposed to do, David?" Tony really liked David and respected him, but for all his acceptance, he couldn't really know how they felt. "You said it yourself. We don't stand a Jew's chance in Auschwitz of fighting the first issue, let alone *this*."

David wasn't giving up; he hated to see anyone allow an injustice, as if one little one didn't matter. "Funny you should mention Auschwitz. Hitler tried to wipe out the Gay population in Europe as well as the Jews."

"I don't *need* a history lesson, Mary." Tony was getting his lip out of joint.

David glared at him as if to say that a history lesson was precisely what he did need. But he softened a little as he turned to Elizabeth. "There must be some way."

Tony picked up the thread. "Shit, Elizabeth. If they fired every Gay person on campus, they'd have to close the school."

David looked skeptical. "Come on, Tony. There aren't *that* many."

"More than you think, Gracie. And I'm only counting the certified ones."

Elizabeth sighed heavily. "That invisible army of ours is hardly going to come thundering out of the closet to *my* coming out party. And I don't want one anyway."

She glanced at Tony as he dropped his eyes, embarrassed and ashamed. He had thought he'd do anything for her. Thundering out hadn't been something he'd included in *anything*.

She realized how he'd taken what she'd said; softly she touched his cheek. "Oh, Sugar, I didn't mean it that way. Of course you can't. I'd never ask it. Or expect it. I understand your choice not to join that parade."

David's voice was quiet and intense in a way Elizabeth and Tony had never heard him. As though he understood much more than they realized.

"Define choice, Elizabeth."

* * *

Curtis didn't look at her directly anymore and rarely spoke. When he had to, it was almost as if nothing had happened. But behind his carefully constructed behavior, Elizabeth could sense something else. He was pleased with himself, but somehow surprised at the same time. And at first, there was a tiny hint of embarrassment, but that had disappeared like the hole made in water by a tossed stone.

Then there was Chuck. His arrogance seemed even more inflated, and she found herself twisting in mental acrobatics just to keep from having to use her already dwindling energy in avoiding him. And this, she knew, was using twice as much.

She had gone over the situation again and again until her thoughts turned back on themselves like exposed entrails. Everywhere she looked was a poor choice, no solution that both rescued her principles and her privacy.

There was only one person to whom she could turn who had both power and compassion. Elizabeth couldn't be sure there'd be any shade this time, but she was in a desert. She had to try. And finally she had to believe the thousands of facets of herself that she had shown to Dr. Harrison would not be shattered into worthlessness by the one that she'd kept turned away. Her flaws were visible through any of them, not just this one. And like any other facet, it had power, the power to reflect, so that people could see something of themselves on its surface. And mirrors don't please even ten percent of the time. Sometimes they frighten. Or lead to other worlds.

Dinner was as good as excuse as any, and they owed her one anyway. Kincaid outdid herself, to the point of having everything ready concurrently. She wouldn't let Elizabeth do anything, knowing she would probably drop something or cut herself. Kincaid knew that if Elizabeth went through with this, it would be like presenting this information to her mother. Again. Elizabeth wouldn't have told her mother at all if she hadn't felt forced to. Not forced exactly, but she had split up with her first lover, a stormy, angry, shattering event which had nearly broken Elizabeth. She stayed on the verge of tears for weeks and lost her patience over nothing. She knew her mother well enough to know that she would think it was somehow something that she had done to Elizabeth. Elizabeth adored her parents and wanted them to know that her depression had nothing to do with them, and that she wasn't going to do anything foolish, like snacking on too many Valiums. Her mother dealt with the news remarkably well. She didn't like the idea of it, but she didn't like to think about sex of any kind, much less when it was Elizabeth's. She loved Elizabeth though, and loved Kincaid and had become pretty successful at not thinking about the rest of it.

When Kincaid had told her own mother, Mrs. Phillips had said calmly, "I know, dear. Pass the butter." That did not ensure a similar response from anyone else. Without a lot of practice, coming out is brand new every time you do it.

So Elizabeth sat at the table with Kincaid and Dr. Harrison and teased her food and wrestled with her decision, never made until it saw the light of day by peeking out her mouth.

Dr. Harrison knew something was hiding in the conversation and at first thought it might have been something she'd said or done. She finally decided to enjoy Kincaid's dinner; she knew Elizabeth would unveil the hidden agenda only when she was ready.

Kincaid steered the conversation around like the captain of a schooner through a coral reef, keeping the bow pointed resolutely toward Dr. Harrison, who pretended ignorance of the voyage.

"My publisher insists on my last chapter by February. A real Simon Legree . . . or was that Schuster?" Dr. Harrison smiled at her author's esoterica.

"Your tenth book," Kincaid said admiringly. "A celebrated author in our very midst."

Dr. Harrison smiled but she sensed butter being applied to her ego. But then, she liked butter on her ego. "They're just history texts, Kincaid. Not exactly a best seller." She insisted on perspective even in flattery.

"They are, too," Kincaid protested. "You're famous."

"In some circles. The dusty, stodgy ones." Dr. Harrison took a bite of beef burgundy and chewed slowly, silently looking at Elizabeth, who smiled and looked at her plate. "You've been awfully quiet, young lady. You haven't told me a thing about your progress with Dr. Curtis." Patience was one thing, infinity another.

Elizabeth glanced over her wine glass at Kincaid, who stared encouragingly back at her over hers. Elizabeth swallowed hard. "There . . . hasn't been much progress."

Following Elizabeth's eyes to Kincaid, she tried to read each face, then responded, a professor hearing an incorrect answer. "Hasn't *been* much? Why not?"

Again, Elizabeth looked at Kincaid, then down at her plate, her domestic rice now almost wild from teasing. "It's gotten . . . a little more . . . complicated than I'd expected."

Dr. Harrison watched Elizabeth, who watched Kincaid, who watched Dr. Harrison, then her wine, then Elizabeth.

"Is there a ball bouncing around on this table, or what, ladies? You can't keep your eyes still. Why do you keep looking at Kincaid, Elizabeth? Is she supposed to be providing you with the answers?"

"She's making every effort," Elizabeth said ironically.

"Will you *please* tell me what's going on?" Again Elizabeth looked to Kincaid. "Stop *doing* that," Dr. Harrison said impatiently, glancing suspiciously from one to the other. "I don't enjoy mysteries."

"You said you were going to tell her tonight," Kincaid said softly to Elizabeth. "She can't help if you don't."

Elizabeth hesitated and took a breath, her heart beginning to race. As she raised her wine glass to her lips, Dr. Harrison could see her hand trembling. "I don't . . . have much practice at this, Jeanette . . . don't know any easy way to slide into this topic gracefully."

Dr. Harrison saw Elizabeth's trembling hand and stifled her impulse to cover it with her own. But her voice was almost as soothing as a mother's touch, as much softness as she would allow herself. "Just say it, Elizabeth. We'll correct your snytax later."

Elizabeth took in a long breath and searched Kincaid's face, then Dr. Harrison's. Finally her eyes steadied but not her hands, nor her heart. "Kincaid and I . . . Jeanette . . . we're . . . not just . . . roommates. We're lovers, Jeanette."

Dr. Harrison looked evenly at her, then to Kincaid. She picked up her wine and took a long gulp that seemed to catch in her throat. Elizabeth held her breath. Dr. Harrison dabbed the wine from her upper lip with the linen napkin and cleared her throat. She looked almost insulted.

"You must think, young lady, that I'm not very . . . observant." Her voice was strangely gentle, firmly maternal, as if her prize student had told her, as a sparkling revelation, the date of the Battle of Hastings.

Now Elizabeth felt almost foolish like she had been trying to keep World War II a secret. "I didn't think we were . . . obvious."

"I may be an old woman, Elizabeth. But I have not yet reached senility. Even from my ivory cloisters I can recognize love when I see it."

Kincaid touched Elizabeth's fingertips, then slid her palm over her hand. "I told you it'd be OK. Your friends are your friends."

Their hands together were suddenly all Jeanette could see; the light diffused, and she careened across time forty years and saw other hands. Then other smiles, other touches, soft amber light and lavender skies. Millay's poems and a woman's laughter caught her like waves that washed across her eyes and drew faces on a shore in her mind, the moon setting full and softly silver.

Elizabeth watched. And saw without seeing, without naming but knowing how to call.

When Jeanette looked up into Elizabeth's eyes, it was as though she looked through a piece of stained glass, cloudy and softly colored. Elizabeth saw eyes that were sad and distant, eyes that blinked at her as if regaining consciousness, eyes that finally and with effort began to focus.

"Fred found out." Elizabeth said softly.

"Yes," Jeanette called, sounding leagues away, but approaching with reluctant gruffness. "Complicated. I see."

Hours later, the flames in Elizabeth's fireplace were low with hardly any fuel or heat, and their flicker reflected on Jeanette's glasses as she stared into the fire. Elizabeth leaned against Kincaid's knees, everyone watching the flames as if an answer lay near the ashes.

Jeanette blew out her breath with an exhausted huff at the details Elizabeth had just finished. "What pleasant choices Curtis offers: Would you like a rock, a piece of granite or a hard spot?" She hesitated, struggling, keeping herself once-removed from questions against which she'd thought herself insulated. Even now, she saw her kinship to this problem as a distant cousin to it. She was not like Elizabeth and Kincaid, not like them.

It was a long time ago; it was only once, with only one woman. She was not like them.

"You obviously can't take him to court now, Elizabeth. You must think of your career. And yours, Kincaid."

"This *is* my career, Jeanette. And what kind of career does she have now, with Curtis acting like the master puppeteer?" Kincaid had made up her mind to tell her ex-husband about her relationship with Elizabeth, and she no longer could see the value in all this stalling around. Once Kincaid decided that an action was correct, she thought everybody else ought to fall in behind her in the parade she had organized, whether or not they were dressed for the occasion, had arrived at the appropriate street, or even recognized the event they were supposed to be celebrating.

Elizabeth caught a spark from Kincaid as well as from a smoldering fire inside herself. "The more I think about him the madder I get. He has no right!"

"You can't let your anger ruin your reason, Elizabeth," Dr. Harrison said, forever convinced that reason had nothing to do with emotions.

"We can't let fear ruin it either." Kincaid knew that reason and emotion were inseparable neighbors who argued across a common fence between houses from which neither could move.

"Just let me think about this for a while. It doesn't have to be an all-or-nothing proposition." But Jeanette was aware, if only vaguely, that this wasn't completely true, that diverting energy expended energy. The choices were not whether it was spent, but how. And she had been building dams for forty years. There was one reservoir that she could tap however. She would call Geoffrey Meade. She couldn't tell the president everything, but surely he would help Elizabeth simply because she asked him to without requiring all these superfluous details. Surely thirty years of trust and respect were worth one unquestioned favor. She detested asking for favors, but she would do it for Elizabeth.

* * *

Dog was waiting on her when Jeanette walked tiredly through her back door and Dog's fuzzy head got an automatic caress. Dog followed Jeanette down the hall and into her study, and watched her reach among the piles of books and papers on her desk for a certain volume. From the only bare spot on the desk, she lifted her leather volume of Millay.

The book fell open in her hands to the spot where she kept the photograph. Two bright and almost innocent young faces looked at each other with no possibility of hiding the truth of their feelings from each other or anyone else who took the time to look.

Gently, she traced the ragged scar that ran between the two of them on the once-torn picture. The book and the picture and her memories were yellowing now and fragile, almost brittle. But even if the photograph dissolved with time, Jeanette knew she'd always know those eyes, would see them in her sleep, would find them after death.

She touched the picture with two gentle fingers, as if finding her lover again in a mist, and she brought her fingers to her lips. She bowed her head and sighed heavily. Dear God. If only it could have been different. If only, if only. The most desolate phrase in the entire language. She replaced the photograph, closed the book and slid it back into its place on a high shelf. Dog's eyes followed her to the brandy decanter and watched her pour an unusually large amount.

She took a sip of resolve and then another and clenched her jaw. Stop this, she told herself. You will not be maudlin, and you will not think about this again. It was different. We were different. We were impossible. Impossible things, by definition, don't exist.

She sighed again, but deeply and quick, like a sneeze of the mind, clearing her thoughts of dust. She downed the brandy, took off her glasses and rubbed the little pink footprints where they had rested.

Dog followed her up the stairs to the bedroom. For the thousandth time, Dog wished she had arms so she could console this woman. Though she knew it wouldn't help, because Jeanette wouldn't have allowed herself to be held.

* * *

Inside Lisa's car, a battle was raging. Actually, several battles. The one in Lisa's brain. The one in Jake's. And the one between them, the one that Lisa felt she'd been drafted for and wasn't sure she could win.

Jake covered Lisa's mouth wetly with his and began exploring with his tongue. Lisa pulled away, and he went back dejectedly to the first line of attack: soft little nibbles on her neck and ears and then her lips until she sighed. But every time she sighed, he got carried away and assumed she had consented to his ultimate intent.

"Jake . . . please," she struggled against him again, his hand moving insistently between the buttons of her blouse. "I'm afraid . . . please . . . don't—"

He covered her mouth again and his tongue shot inside, then out and over her lips. She heard his zipper and felt him move in the seat, his hand sliding from inside her blouse to the back of her head, and he began to push her head toward his lap. She strained against his hand. He pushed harder.

"This won't hurt you, baby," he gasped, his other hand exploring roughly between her legs. "Relax, just relax." He wasn't taking his own advice.

"Damn it," she hissed between her teeth. She put one hand against his arm and one against his chest and shoved. "*Stop* it!"

Jake collapsed in an angry, frustrated heap behind the wheel, spitting expletives. He glared at Lisa, tucked himself awkwardly back into his pants and zipped them shut with a dangerous jerk.

"Goddamnit, Lisa! I don't know what the *hell* you want!"

"Well, not *this*!" She was just as mad, snatching her clothes back into some facsimile of order.

"What's the *matter* with *this*? You think you can go through your whole life and not have to do anything but *kiss* a guy?" He fumed and tried to adjust his unadjustable self through his jeans. "Grow up!"

Growing up was what she was trying to do, but she failed to see that this particular activity had anything to do with it. Yet somehow when anyone told her to grow up, it made her feel little. She had tried to explain to Jake about her fear of pregnancy, how she couldn't have either a child or an abortion, that she refused to use the chemicals or devices that might prevent one thing but cause another. And this was the solution he proposed. She wanted him to understand and be patient. He wanted her to understand that he *had* been.

"I like it when you're gentle with me, Jake," she said softly. "But you always change." She didn't want to stay mad and didn't want him to. She couldn't stand for people to be mad at her.

"Well, you're the *first* one who didn't like it," he spat at her, his voice icy with hurt, his patience a commodity in short supply.

Tears began in her eyes, and she looked away in the dark, trying not to let them fall. "Let's go, Jake," she said even more softly. "Let's just go."

He looked disgustedly at her, jerked the door open and hauled himself out. He slammed the door as hard as he could and glowered in the window at her. "*You* go! Goddamn prick teaser! I need some fresh air! Among other things!"

Lisa looked back at him, hot tears of anger now in her eyes. She climbed out the passenger side and rounded the car in three strides. She jerked the door open, herself inside and the engine on in almost a single motion. She slammed the door shut as hard as he had and laid rubber down twenty feet of the narrow road.

Jake watched the taillights disappear, and they seemed to match the two hot coals in his head that he watched them with. He began to curse and to murder a small clump of weeds, his foot a cold-blooded pendulum in the dust.

What the hell was he supposed to do? He had never felt this way about a girl before. Sure, he wanted to be next to her, to touch her, to make love to her, just like he had with the rest of them. But it was different with Lisa. He hadn't known he had wanted it to be different until just now. He stared at the diminishing taillights and kicked the clump of weeds again. Then he reached up and angrily wiped away the tears that had somehow appeared on his face.

Let him walk, damn him, Lisa thought as she sped by the campus. Not that far anyway. Can't talk to him. Won't listen. Doesn't care about *my* life. What *I* want to do. Damn him. Thinks all I should be interested in are *his* damn football stories, or *his* old girlfriends or *his* plans. His, his, his. She stomped on the accelerator and shot onto the freeway, driving blindly, wiping away tears on her sleeve only to have another, hotter one course down her face.

But gradually the tears slowed and so did the car, though her driving was as aimless as her thoughts. She didn't know what to do about Jake. She liked him, cared about him. But.

There was always a *but*. And when she got to the *but*, she couldn't see any farther, as if someone had built a wall or a dam, and she couldn't see over it.

Then she saw the exit sign above the highway, the one she hadn't known she'd been looking for. Three more turns and a stop sign and Lisa pulled in front of Elizabeth's home, silent and dark like Lisa herself. Lisa cut the engine and sat for a long time looking at the ornately carved front door. All she could hear were the last persistent October insects, the die-hards from summer who noisily insisted the seasons not change. Then she turned the key and slowly drove away.

* * *

"You're stalling again." Elizabeth watched the woman pace around her office, exploring contents that she must already know by heart.

Martha picked a small dried flower from an arrangement on Elizabeth's desk and looked at Elizabeth all curled in a tired knot in her wingback. She crossed to the couch and sank into its deep cushions, twirling the flower between her thumb and finger and studying the botanic propeller as if it were the reason she'd come in there.

"I don't know how to start," Martha stalled.

"No kidding."

Martha didn't look up, but she knew Elizabeth was smiling. "I've done a bad thing," she insisted.

"I doubt it."

"No, really. I overheard, that is, I eavesdropped on a conversation in the office. More than a week ago."

This sounded serious and not like Martha at all. Elizabeth looked at her intently and waited.

"Between you and Dr. Curtis. Last Monday afternoon. In his office."

Elizabeth didn't move. Now it begins, she thought.

Martha took a deep breath and finally looked up at Elizabeth. "I've thought about it and thought about it. And I can't keep quiet any more, Elizabeth," she said firmly. Her eyes locked on Elizabeth; the propeller stopped. "He's a sonofabitch, you know. And I just wanted you to know that, well, he's a sonofabitch and you shouldn't let him get away with it." Martha stumbled over the epithet because cursing embarrassed her. But it was the only word she could think of that fit.

Elizabeth still held her breath. "Did you hear the whole conversation?"

Martha smirked. "Every syllable." Then she hesitated, thinking she needed some absolution. "He must have hit his intercom with his size twelves. Clumsiest man I've ever seen."

"It's true, you know." Elizabeth's voice was low.

"About *Lisa*?" Martha's eyes popped open.

Elizabeth's eyes popped to match. "No! Not that part!"

Martha settled back into righteousness and gunned her propeller. "The rest of it's none of his or anybody else's business. Who you live with's got nothing to do with your job."

She gently touched Martha's shoulder and shook her head sadly. "It does now."

"Oh, poot. For pity's sake, Elizabeth." Martha was getting fired up now. When she said *poot*, it was about to hit the fan. "If you ask me, uninvited folks who spend their time getting upset about other people's private lives, well, they must have nasty, mean little lives of their own to match their nasty, mean little minds. And *that's* what they *ought* to be worrying about." She took a breath, tuning up like a TV sermonette. "This kind of stuff happens so often around here, you'd think it came as a directive from the Board of Trustees." She saw Elizabeth's surprised look. "I mean power plays, manipulation. Gossip. Control. Bowing down to the Almighty Status Quo. Well, I'm not going to be party to it another minute. I think it's time for somebody *else* to kick a little hind quarter around here. And in some other direction than from the top down!"

* * *

The clock behind Jeanette's mountainously piled desk measured the morning at 8:02. She gripped the phone receiver as if it might escape and was not pleased at what she was hearing.

"Out of the country? Well, when will he be back?" she mashed her lips against each other as she waited. "No, that won't do at all. I have to speak with President Meade in person. Can you give me no earlier appointment? Of *course*, I want an exception made! Who doesn't? Oh, all right. But if someone ahead of me dies, move me up."

She punched the button in the cradle, waited a moment and dialed four digits.

"Elizabeth? Jeanette. No. I couldn't. He's in France with some alumni group. Due back the end of the week." She looked puzzled, then tensed her jaw. "Martha? Your secretary . . .?" She listened impatiently "I *know* she's not *yours*. I didn't call to discuss the merits of private property . . . I see. Well, I really won't need to discuss any of that with Dr. Meade. It really is beside the point, isn't it?"

She listened a few seconds. "Believe me, Elizabeth. Dr. Meade is a reasonable man. Just be patient. Surely it can't be completely unbearable. What can you gain by confronting Curtis?"

* * *

If she had to sit in this office listening to these two insufferable twits another minute, Elizabeth thought she'd explode. Right here in front of God and Adam's house cat. Curtis droned on, talking to her while his eyes never left Chuck.

"I know you've done a lot of work on this project, Lizbuth . . . your idea and all. But Chuck, here, is real enthusiastic about it. You know, exhorbitant. And a real team player. You won't mind, I'm sure, if he picks up the ball and carries it from here, now will you, Lizbuth?" He finally looked at her for the briefest second. His expression resembled Chuck's, and they both looked as though they were enjoying the recent demise of an imagined canary.

How could they not see what she was screaming in her mind? How could they not hear her eyes?

Sonofabitch, she fumed in her mind, reduced now to old habits and barbarous words learned in childhood, Anglo-Saxon plosives that fired from her lips like bullets.

* * *

"Sonofabitch!" Elizabeth exploded. The cat leaped from the bed and darted under the dresser.

"Right," Kincaid said softly, not looking up from the law journal in her hand.

"That idiot is *crazy* if he thinks I'll let Chuck Gardner take credit for *my* work and *my* ideas!" She lay propped up on a stack of pillows next to Kincaid, her arms crossed and her attitude way the hell out of joint.

"Right."

"I'll quit first!"

Kincaid lowered the journal slowly and looked over the top of it at Elizabeth, whose steam was almost visible. Kincaid knew that when Elizabeth got this way, which was about as often and as significant as a lunar eclipse, she was wise to keep her own voice calm and her emotions under rein. But she refused to let that be a censor.

"There's another choice, Elizabeth. There's telling the truth."

Elizabeth clenched her teeth. "Damn it, Kincaid! Will you *stop* with your high and mighty *cause*." She turned to stare at her lover as if Kincaid had grown a beard. "The truth?! You want to know what the *truth* is? What it's always been for every *queer* who ever drew breath?" Hers was hissing now like a leopard. "The truth is needing a simple thing called *being liked*. It's parents who's *best* response is embarrassment! It's one thing for *them* to know; it's another for them to have to explain it to their bridge club! And it's money! A job! The reason this whole damn thing started in the first place."

"This whole damn thing started, dearest, when you were *four* years old and madly in love with Nancy Whitehall. I've *seen* her picture. She *couldn't* have been worth all this." Kincaid's tone reeked of sarcasm, and she stared at Elizabeth until her lover looked away. Elizabeth saw no sense in a test of wills when a draw was the only conclusion possible. She blew out a long sigh and with it some of her anger, and looked entreatingly back at Kincaid, then away.

"Why is it everyone's so ready for *me* to strap on the gloves? All of you people see these almighty big *issues*. All I see are almighty big *consequences*." She turned toward the headboard and tortured her pillows into another shape. "People who want *me* to storm the beaches won't *have* any consequences. Or can't see there *are* any." She cut her eyes toward Kincaid pointedly and flounced back on her pillows.

"You'll have consequences no matter what you do. One of them is to continue this schizophrenic existence."

The word cut through Elizabeth like a rusty scalpel, and her eyes closed from the painful, old, ragged truth of it. Silently she opened them, looking at her hands. Watching her, Kincaid's eyes and tone softened, but not her intention.

"It's not just us you're concerned about, anyway. Is it?"

Elizabeth glanced at her and saw that familiar mind-reader's look. It was spooky sometimes. "There is no way I'm going to involve Lisa in this. She's *not* involved except in that *pervert's* mind."

"We won't mention her. He won't dare. However he got those notes, they were stolen. He's dumber than I think if he even hints at them or her. He can't out-maneuver me."

"This isn't a naval exercise, damn it!" Elizabeth flared.

Kincaid bit the inside of her lip to keep from flaring back and took a deep breath. Then a spark of devilment twinkled in her eye and she poked Elizabeth in her naked abdomen.

"But there's nothing worse than a flabby navel, doncha know." She sounded like Sophie Tucker. Or Bette Midler doing Sophie Tucker.

Elizabeth couldn't help herself. It was impossible to stay mad at her when Kincaid was like this. She sputtered a little laugh through lips that were losing their grip on each other, and her anger was gone. Kincaid laughed, too, and then spoke softly.

"You're not in this alone, Angel. But as long as people can make us hide, they can make us feel alone. Can make us seem sick, even evil. Invisible people are easy to lie about. And to hate."

Elizabeth absorbed it all still watching her hands, a decision still out of reach. Kincaid watched her face, took Elizabeth's hands in hers and brought them to her lips, kissing the fingertips.

"Shall we be alone forever? Always in the dark? Will it always be as painful as it was for you and me?" Kincaid asked softly. "You know who gives the blackmailer his power. The victims. The victims do."

Slowly Elizabeth raised her eyes and then her hands to cup Kincaid's face. And in her eyes was a decision. Elizabeth held one hand toward Kincaid, palm up.

"Gimme two," she said softly.

And gently, smiling, Kincaid touched the two fingertips with two of her own.

* * *

In the court clerk's office, a long line of three-piece tweed and herringbone suits moved slowly forward, documenting their quota of legal and illegal activities. Kincaid's tweed was among them, and while she waited, she didn't hear the soap opera being played out at a young female clerk's desk fifty feet away. Kincaid knew the reporter that sat on the clerk's desk, intently pursuing several agenda, so knew the gist of at least one of them. It was listed under *B* for *bedroom*. Kincaid was in the wrong column. He had passed *B* and was in *C* for *Connive*.

"Come on, honey. Give a guy a break. I need a story today. Something juicy, ya know. My editor's sick of divorces and robberies and cliché crimes." He stroked the clerk's pencil for emphasis.

The clerk pouted disappointedly. She was still in column *B*. "I thought you wanted to take me to dinner. Among other places. All you care about is your damn newspaper."

"Oh, baby, that's not true. But you could save me a lot of time. Save us both some. For other things." He winked. "You see nearly every case that comes through here. You're a smart girl. You know what I want."

And she did. In every column. But she liked the third column the best and was determined to become the recipient of its contents, long and heinous.

Kincaid moved up in line to the clerk in front of her and handed him two sets of legal documents. He smiled at her, looked her up and down appreciatively and stamped the two folders. Handing one back to her, he dropped the other in a wire basket on his desk.

Kincaid turned to leave as the reporter looked up and smiled at her, a conquest he had dogged for years and who steadfastly failed to recognize his merits. He waved to Kincaid.

"Hey, John," she called, friendly but preoccupied as usual.

* * *

President Geoffrey Meade's office looked like one decorated for the corporate chairman of the board that he was. The budget and the personnel and the politics that he oversaw were as huge and as complex as any company's. Moreso. Because his was publicly owned in a more direct sense than any company, and the people he juggled and balanced included the governor and the state legislature, the alumni, the citizens and the faculty, and most complex of all, the football fans.

Across one wall in the darkly paneled and plush office were testimonies to his citizenship, his scholarship and his leadership. Across another, richly bound matching volumes that looked as if they were there for decoration, except that he'd read them all. A third wall was glass, a huge window that framed the campus like an architect's rendering.

In front of him sat Jeanette Harrison, as formidable now as she had been thirty years ago. And if possible, even sharper. He respected her more than most men he knew, but she was asking the impossible now.

"Go through *channels*?!" Jeanette almost shouted. "You're the president of this institution! You *are* the channels!"

He remained calm, although he knew that whoever had gotten her revved up had better have a bomb shelter handy. And he was glad it wasn't him she was after; she still scared him a little, made him feel he was back in the front row of her classroom.

"Now, Jeanette. Be reasonable. You know how things work around here. I may be the president, but I haven't been around here long enough to tell Paul Thompson what to do with his people."

Jeanette was formidable, but she was his friend, former mentor and current ally. Paul Thompson had no friends; he had donors and endowments and pledges and he had to be handled carefully. Meade knew Thompson envied him his position even though he hadn't applied for it. It was rumored that Thompson had been incensed because he had not been invited to apply for the presidency, and not being invited, knew he couldn't win. Meade didn't want to view his dealings with Thompson or anyone else as a contest, but since they did, he had to, to some degree. You had to use channels, else why have anyone else working there? But that was the whole purpose of having bosses. They were of absolutely no use unless someone down the line was irresponsible, inept or overburdened. He felt that all three conditions required education and assistance. That's what he said on the lecture circuit, that is. His first reaction when people didn't do their jobs was anger. But he always tried to get the facts so that when he landed with both feet on somebody, he was sure it was the guilty body. Jeanette knew this about him, and investigation was the very thing she wanted to circumvent.

"If you depend on Paul Thompson to determine a woman's station in life, we'd all be in maternity dresses and the women's shoe industry would be bankrupt!" She stormed around the office like a tiger with its tail on fire. "Am I the one and only soul on this campus who's not afraid of being strangled by that man's purse strings?"

"That was not nice, Jeanette . . . I believe it was in your class that I learned the relationship between discretion and valor. And in any case, I would have to investigate the circumstances. There might be some reason for—"

"*Reason*?!" Jeanette was full throttle now. "What you need to investigate, Geoffrey Meade, is a system that allows a Fred Curtis to draw breath with its blessing! I've *seen* you when you get mad at injustice and I'm *telling* you it's time to get mad!"

"Lord in heaven, Jeanette. Why is Elizabeth McKay so important to you? Frankly, I'm surprised you're not letting her fend for herself. I wish you'd gotten this wrought up over *my* salary. Sometimes I think you have more influence around here than I do."

His intercom buzzed as he took a breath. "You see how powerful I am? I can't even convince my secretary to hold my calls." He picked up the receiver and punched a button. "Yes . . .? No. You did the right thing. I'll talk to him. What's his name again?" There was no joking in his voice now and the tense, almost angry look he shot at Jeanette stopped her in mid-thought.

"This is Geoffrey Meade. Can I help you?" he said into the phone. His face grew graver as he listened, and he watched Jeanette as if somehow she were the subject under discussion. "Yes, she's a psychologist in our student counseling center." Meade's tense eyes locked on Jeanette's. "I'm not aware of any law suit." He paused, listening. "You may assure the readers of your paper, sir, that whatever things the University condones, blackmail isn't one of them. No comment. No. No comment . . . You're welcome."

He hung up the phone, his eyes never leaving Jeanette's. "How well did you think you knew this protegé of yours, Jeanette?" Not waiting for her answer, which didn't exist in any event, he punched his intercom. "Get Sam Fitzhugh up here. *Now*."

* * *

Fred Curtis heaved himself to his breakfast table, sleep still clinging stickily to his eyes, and reached beyond his heaped plate for his coffee and the morning paper. He and his wife had both spent their lives trying to help the starving children of India, China and Europe by vacuuming their own plates. Now Curtis was having to do it for both of them, because he had insisted his wife go on another, not visibly successful, diet.

She stared in boredom and disappointment at her dry toast as he handed her the paper minus the sports section. Reading at the table with her husband had always presented a unique problem for her, because he ate louder than she could think. It took all of her considerable powers of concentration to tune out what sounded like a cow repeatedly and unsuccessfully removing its foot from a mud slide.

She skimmed the front page without much interest or success as Curtis slurped and smacked his way through the NFL recap. Then her eyes locked on a small article near the bottom, between the Palestinian question, the arms control question, two murders and a rape. The further she read, the further her jaw dropped. When she found the rest of the story somewhere inside the paper, her eyelids shot open and she clutched the throat of her dressing gown.

"Freddie!" she shouted, shoving the paper at him and jabbing frantically at it.

He peered around his section at her, annoyed but not surprised. She did this same thing over the Sears ads. He pulled the page from her, then glanced down solemnly to the headline.

"Lesbian Psychologist Sues University," it screamed silently at him. The blood began to drain from his forehead, and he felt as if bees were all inside him trying to escape.

"Pay Discrimination, Blackmail Charged," the page harked and heralded.

Sweat popped out around his horrified eyes, and he swallowed what he was sure would be his final morsel on earth, because he intended on having a stroke in about five minutes. His eyes moved almost of their own accord, as if he were passing carnage on the highway or watching the shower scene in *Psycho*.

"Although blackmail is a criminal offense continued on page A-3 oh shit oh shit," Curtis read and searched frantically for the elusive A-3, "oh shit oh shit oh the suit was filed as a civil matter and no arrests are expected." He knew it was coming; he saw his name and read backwards from it.

"The suit however, charges the University with pay discrimination, specifically accusing Dr. Fred Curtis with attempting to prevent the plaintiff from seeking salary equity by allegedly threatening to dismiss her because of her sexual orientation." Not exactly Alfred Hitchcock material, but it was the most convincing horror story he'd ever read.

Next to him on the wall, the phone blasted into his ear, setting off a small explosion under his butt and launching him three inches into the air.

"Hello," he said meekly, his sweat beginning to sweat. "Well . . . I was . . . planning to . . . come in, yes." He gulped. "Then . . . I won't, uh, no . . . sir. Yes, sir. Two o'clock, Wednesday. Your office. Yes, sir. Well, yes, but . . . Yes, sir."

His eyes glazed as he hung up the phone and reached for the paper again, hoping the print had disappeared, that a black hole had sucked it into infinity and might soon mercifully come for him. His wife began to feed her anxiety from his forgotten plate as the sick expression on his face lapsed into one that was critically ill, then terminal.

* * *

Jake sat in the deafening cafeteria, drumming his fingers on the front page of the paper and smiling to himself. He laced his hands behind his head, stuck his long, muscular legs under the table and stretched. Across the room he saw Lisa come out of the serving area, carrying a loaded tray and looking around for a place to sit.

He hesitated, then stood and yelled her name above the din. She stopped looked at him a moment, then headed for his table, though she was hardly hurrying.

Patting the seat next to him, he smiled up at her and pushed his tray out of her way.

"Howya been?" he said, looking for something to eat from her plate. He grabbed a piece of lettuce and popped it in his mouth.

She shrugged. "OK. You?"

He shrugged. Sparkling conversation, he thought. He drummed his fingers on the paper. "Wha'd'ya think of your idol now?"

"Who?" said Lisa, knowing who he meant but not what.

He pushed the paper over to her and tapped his finger next to the article. She saw only the headline and Elizabeth's name before the page blurred completely, and her mind went numb. Something in her froze.

"It's not true," she whispered. "It can't be."

"Yeah," Jake yawned. "Sure doesn't look like a dyke."

"She's not a dyke!" Lisa flared. Heads turned everywhere, staring at them.

"Ex-cu-u-use me-e-e!"

She glanced around and lowered her voice. "Don't call her that! You don't even know her."

"What are *you* so up in the air about? I didn't write the story. It says right here she admitted it. Jeez." Then his eyes narrowed as an infuriating thought presented itself. "Hey. She ever try anything with you? 'Cause if she did—" He left the sentence hanging threateningly.

"No!" Lisa said too loudly. "No," she said again, her eyes strangely distant, almost sad. Jake watched her, sorry now that he'd been the one to tell her. Her eyes made his arms hurt, made them ache along the inside as though they were irreparably empty.

He pushed the paper aside and touched her knee softly. "Forget about her, Lisa. It doesn't matter. You didn't need her anyway." He moved his hand further up her leg, and she looked at him, seemed even to be listening to him. "Look, about the other night." He dropped his eyes, then his head. "I'm sorry, Lisa. Really. You know I care about you. I just can't help myself sometimes."

It wouldn't have mattered what else he'd said. She was a million miles away by then. But she held his hand and smiled vaguely, her eyes moving slowly from one thought to another.

Out on the mall a crowd was gathering. The campus paper, as hungry for a juicy item as the next soul, starving actually, had snatched up the story and had run it as the lead. Quick to organize, a small but determined group of students dug out their all-purpose Gay Pride Week placards and marched silently, angrily around in front of the Student Center. The most radical among them wore black armbands with a pink triangle stitched to each, although hardly anyone but they were aware of the patch's historical significance in Hitler's concentration camps. Like the yellow Star of David, they were badges now of honor, not shame. To these few who wore them, anyway.

As Lisa and Jake came out the front door, Jake spotted his wide receiver, Scooter, at the edge of the crowd. Scooter had a strange look on his face, a little frightened, even a little embarrassed, defensive. Jake wasn't watching Scooter's face as he came up behind him and slapped him on the butt.

"Can you believe these freaks, Scooter?" Jake jabbed him in the ribs and pulled Lisa securely to his side, proof to everyone that he wasn't about to love another man. Not even Scooter. "Hey, faggot-queer," Jake sang out. "Does your daddy know you're here?" He hooted and laughed at his extraordinary poetic ability, slapping Scooter on the back.

As two particularly large marchers walked by, one of them cut his eyes hatefully at Jake, but said nothing. It occurred to Jake that these guys looked just like the men in the Winston ad in the September *Playboy*. But better dressed. He stuck his chin out at them and hugged Lisa tighter.

"Either one of you two faggots ever lay a hand on *me*, and I'll *kill* your ass," Jake sneered.

The two marchers stopped, looked at each other, and one jerked his thumb at Jake. "Do you know any man with such poor taste that he would *want* to touch that piece of cow dung?" They laughed, slapping each other on the back.

Before they could fully enjoy themselves at Jake's expense, Jake hurtled through the air and caught both of them in a flying tackle. Then it was bedlam. Bodies everywhere, fists flying. Everybody who'd wanted to fight all afternoon over any issue at all finally got their chance.

Campus cops, who had been waiting for something to happen again since 1968, hopped into the middle of things, delighted to have at last some factions to separate. Worsted administrators, relieved that a crisis for once wasn't financial, charged down the steps to deputize themselves and feel useful as well as ornamental.

Lisa let herself be pushed further and further from the center as people jockeyed in front of her toward ringside. She stumbled, adrift, disconnected, neither of the crowd nor beyond it.

And in the distance, above it all, Jeanette watched from a classroom window on the top floor of her building. She was barely breathing, but what there was of the air in her nostrils smelled of brimstone. She closed her eyes against the chaos outside and beneath her, and turned her back on the scene, her head falling heavily toward her breast, then back against the window sill. In her mind, a name echoed in a secret, hollow cavern, in fury and pain and horror.

Elizabeth!

* * *

"What, in the name of all that is holy, do you think you've gained by this?" Jeanette raged, so furious she trembled. "And why, Elizabeth, at the very least, didn't you *tell me* what you were going to do? *Before* you did it?"

Jeanette stood in the middle of their living room and glared at Elizabeth, then at Kincaid, then strode to the mantel to hold on to it for support. Elizabeth had known by the tone of her voice on the phone that Jeanette was coming with her teeth bared. Jeanette hadn't asked to come; she had told them to be home when she got there. Elizabeth had often seen Jeanette angry. But not like this. And it frightened her until she felt small and vulnerable.

"I called you, Jeanette. Five times. Left messages. The last time your department office said you were with Dr. Meade." Elizabeth was pleading, but there was not a hint of a crevice in the wall around Jeanette. "Do you think we *wanted* this in the paper? We could have filed criminal charges but didn't. We wanted it settled quietly, out of court. Jeanette, please."

Jeanette's eyes were incisions. "You were just bound and determined, weren't you?" Elizabeth felt her eyes grow hot and full; she looked away.

"Jeanette, reporters don't usually read the details of a civil suit; they're too routine," Kincaid interceded, a little afraid of the professor herself; but then, she didn't love her the way Elizabeth did, and the distance shielded her. "This guy thinks he's Bob Woodward at the *Washington Post*."

Jeanette ignored Kincaid's attempt. "You have no patience! Either of you. And not the slightest sense of form or decorum." She spat the words like bitter herbs. "Not a whit of patience! And I have none for you! It was irresponsible. People could have been hurt today! The University definitely was!"

"Who the *hell* is this *University* you keep talking about?" Kincaid flared. "Elizabeth is as much the University as you are! And we don't need lectures from our *liberal* friends." Kincaid had a mouthful of dill herself. "We can *be* Gay, is that it? But don't *flaunt* it? As long as we look straight, as long as we're *good* little girls. As long as we can *pass for white*!" Kincaid flung this last at her, and it chipped Jeanette between the eyes. Kincaid marked the spot where it had landed, a crack in the wall.

Elizabeth saw her flinch, too. "Kincaid, don't," she said softly. "She tried to help. It's not her fight."

Jeanette stared at Elizabeth for a long time, still in silent fury, but the crack let a dot of light escape, a hint of awareness, a whisper of recognition. She jerked her eyes loose from Elizabeth's and turned her back to them both, fiercely gripping the mantelpiece with both hands. Her face glared back at herself from the mirror, flames from the fire doing a macabre pas de deux on her glasses.

"That's right. It's *not* my fight," she said as much to herself as to them. "The only thing I've *ever* cared for . . . has been teaching . . . *my* University." But in her mind she could see misty, soft eyes and lavender nights indicting her for her lie. The lie scuttled across her eyes, and she knew its name, wouldn't call it, let it slide into the dusk beyond the crevice. "I won't *allow* this destruction! By *one* selfish soul!"

Elizabeth's eyes were helpless as she moved toward the older woman whom she could see slipping further and further away. She could no longer dam the tears, and they washed shining down her face. Jeanette saw them and whirled on her, a fury with a torch.

"And you're *weak*! Tears! You have tears for yourself! None for what you're *doing*!"

Elizabeth was beyond rescue or comfort. Like a child pleading, she reached out toward her. "Jeanette, please." Her voice was tiny as she softly, tentatively touched Jeanette's arm with just the tips of her fingers. In the midst of the fire in Jeanette's mind, a thought flashed, an instant of regret. She'd never touched Elizabeth before. Not once.

"Don't *touch* me!" Jeanette snatched her arm away as if Elizabeth were diseased, her eyes almost wild, recoiling in fear and revulsion, as if she were staring at her own entrails or at Elizabeth's. Suddenly the fire in her eyes was snuffed; and she was freezing, trembling cold and absolutely alone. She turned her back on them.

Elizabeth looked across the chasm and knew her arms weren't long enough, nor her grip tight enough to reach or hold. Her hand fell to her side, exhausted and useless. Hot tears caught in the fire's lightning as she turned and walked slowly past Kincaid.

Kincaid raised her own hand, surely strong enough for Elizabeth, but knew the drop of water she held to soothe this burning tongue was wet with more good intention than relief. She looked at Elizabeth's blinded eyes, then her own empty hand. The futility of it sank in her heart like a lead coffin at sea. She turned back toward Jeanette and saw for an instant that she had been watching Elizabeth's reflection in the mirror. There was something in Jeanette's eyes. And it looked for all the world like remorse. But it fled from her face as she flashed fiery eyes on Kincaid, who steeled her own and her back as Elizabeth walked slowly out of the room.

"She'd have let me handle this if you hadn't pushed her so." Jeanette's voice was low and threatening, tones in it that echoed almost of possession, of jealousy. "Now I *can't* help her! You didn't have to make an issue of it. I could have—"

"Freedom *is* an issue, Jeanette." Kincaid kept her tone as quiet and smooth as barrister training allowed. "We didn't make it one. Chains and ropes you can get without requesting them. Freedom's a little harder to come by." She moved to the mantel, the better to see the woman's eyes which were covered by real and imaginary flames on every side.

"I remember once, Jeanette, we talked about your work in the fifties and sixties for blacks, your marching in Selma and Memphis, your commitment."

"This is hardly the same thing." Impatient and superior, Jeanette clutched at the wood and did not look at Kincaid, who was watching her as if trying to read a hostile witness.

Kincaid's voice was almost gentle now, but so pointed it pierced Jeanette like a lance. "You're right. It's not the same. A white woman could defend blacks, march with them, demand their human rights, condemn the system for its injustice. She might have gotten arrested or called a 'nigger lover.' Or even killed. But she was never . . . ever . . . suspected of being black."

Silence. So long and loud Jeanette's ears rang. She stared into the fire, then released her support and strode to the couch, coldly snatched her purse and jerked opened the front door. On her skin and on her glasses there flickered a strange amber light like the one she had just left. And behind it, surprise and the first sentence of fear.

Kincaid saw it all and took three long strides to the door. The whole yard looked ablaze, then burned itself out almost at once as figures scuttled across the yard and into a waiting car.

In the grass the black, charred stubble shouted in a smoking, angry scrawl of gasoline. DYKE, it screamed at them.

"Dyke!" the men screamed from the car, laughing and celebrating as if they had torched a coven. They gulped whiskey and passed it around as their car roared down the street. One face looked back at the two women, and he stared, his mouth open, recognition forming her name.

Jeanette Harrison had seen Jake Tyler, too, and knew he had seen her. Apprehension is a versatile word, with multiple meanings. In her eyes, all of them huddled, small and constricted.

* * *

PART VI

Jake reached toward the desk chair in front of him, stuck a lighter in front of Lisa's nose and flicked it on. She jumped, not amused, and jerked it out of his hand, cutting her eyes at him to make him behave. Dr. Harrison walked around the classroom returning mid-term exam books and handed Lisa hers. Dr. Harrison was cooler today than usual and it puzzled Lisa. No joking, no laughter and harsh looks for any question, much less a wrong answer. But she looked on the front of her paper and saw in Dr. Harrison's neat, almost Old English script, a large decisive *A*. And beneath it, "Excellent, Lisa. Our graduate program needs you." Lisa beamed and looked at Jake.

Dr. Harrison stood next to him and held out his paper. On it was a letter equally prophetic but hardly encouraging. An *F* shown brightly red under Dr. Harrison's thumb.

Jake sat slouched in his seat, his arms folded, a smile playing at his lips. He didn't move, but merely stared at her. Dr. Harrison's eyes narrowed slightly and she dropped his paper on his desk, looked coldly at him another moment and walked back to the podium as the bell rang.

"If you have any questions about your grade, please make an appointment."

She turned her back to them and hardly looked at anyone who spoke to her; barely noticed Lisa's excitement or how it vanished when her professor didn't smile back at her.

Lisa waited for Jake as the classroom emptied, but still he didn't move, just hulked in his seat like a bored, satiated lion, grinning that enigmatic smile. Finally, he waved her on and she left, puzzled over everything.

Dr. Harrison poked papers and books into her satchel, her rituals forgotten, nothing fitting where it should anymore. She turned to leave and found a football jersey directly in front of her nose.

She stepped back and to the side. "I have a meeting to attend, Mr. Tyler," she said, more tightly than she'd wanted. "Please excuse me."

He stepped back in front of her, smiling but hardly friendly. Everything about him shimmered in a thinly plated coat of menace. "If you flunk me, I'll lose my football scholarship."

She looked at him squarely, not about to be intimidated or not about to let it show. "You *earned* that F, Mr. Tyler. It *wasn't* a gift."

He smirked even more. "Well, I thought since I know so much of *your* history, you might go a little easier on me." He peeled a stick of gum slowly and pushed it in his jaw, knowing she never permitted it in her class and doing it for that reason. He finally knew why he didn't like this woman. He'd been blind not to see it before. It hadn't occurred to him before, because he hadn't considered her in any sexual context, but it was obvious to him now since he had seen her at the house of those other two. Who the hell did she think she was, standing up here all this time lording it over him? Nothing but a dyke. And if she's not, probably wishes she was, because no man would be dumb enough to have her.

"Birds of a feather, ya know?" he said. "Some people might find it real interesting who you socialize with. They might wonder why you're so friendly with a couple of *dykes*."

The word hit her like a slap, and he saw it. He moved his face closer to hers. "It's not like it would cost you anything, Doc. It's just a grade." He watched her face and saw something that he thought was defeat or perhaps realization, and he thought he knew of what. He smiled at the glimmer of his expected victory.

Her voice was so muted he could barely hear her as she nodded slowly. "Just a grade," she said.

* * *

A load of poot, pure-D poot, Martha thought, sitting at her office desk. That's what it is. The place just wasn't any fun anymore since it hit the fan about Elizabeth. To some people, it was worth it, for entertainment value alone. People hadn't had this much to stir about since somebody had paged Dr. Jack Meeoff over the Student Center P.A., and some joker, higher than a kite with chemical assistance, had taken it as some kind of invitation to do so in the main lounge.

Paul Thompson had called both Elizabeth and Curtis and "asked" that they find it "convenient" to take some annual leave for a few days. Kincaid was against it but relented when Elizabeth reminded her that she wasn't the one who'd have to fight through a throng of reporters or gawking students every day. Therapy couldn't be conducted in that sort of atmosphere, and everyone would be better off if she stayed away.

The only reason Martha hadn't been told to stay home as well was because they knew they'd have to close the office if she did. Tony knew it, anyway, and had argued so eloquently that they'd let her stay, but under a gag order from Paul Thompson. "Gag order, poot," she'd cursed. "People think you have to have a Ph.D. degree around here to have any ethics."

Tony had expected to have to double up on clients in order to cover for Elizabeth, and many of her clients were coming to see him. The ones who were required to come as part of some discipline measure still came. But many of Elizabeth's other clients had stopped. Among them, Lisa Hunter. When Martha called her to reschedule and tell her Tony was covering for Elizabeth, Lisa's voice sounded tense, distant, and she refused an appointment with anyone, and hung up abruptly.

Ever since the story had hit the papers, Chuck had been strutting around like he'd been put in charge. He wasn't, of course, because months before Curtis had designated Tony as Acting Assistant Dean whenever anything required Curtis' absence. The fact that Elizabeth had seniority over Tony and in a sense over Curtis himself was not something Curtis considered. Even at the office inheritance fell to the eldest male heir, but being in charge didn't please Tony much under the circumstances.

Tony was moping around like he'd lost his best friend, which of course he had, or so Martha thought. This whole story was all very confusing to her so she stopped thinking about it. Her own sex life was sufficient in and of itself, and she didn't have the energy to ponder the intricacies of everyone else's.

Here Tony was again, moping around her desk between appointments. He missed Elizabeth, missed seeing her every day. And felt guilty as crime because he couldn't do anything to help. Or wasn't doing anything. But what could he do? Waltz into Thompson's office in pink tights and throw them all on the mercy of the executioner?

Oh, lord, now here comes Chuck, Tony thought. Tony didn't know exactly what part this peacock had played in Elizabeth's dilemma, but he knew Chuck had sided with Curtis, which put him in the dead center of the enemy camp. Tony headed for his office, having successfully avoided Chuck all week. Chuck was the kind of man Tony had studiously postponed becoming, although they had much of the same raw material in common. But Tony thought it a huge weakness to think that looks, brains or money were adequate substitutes for sensitivity. He believed that in all things quantitative there was nothing equal between any two people. But in pain and anger and fear, everyone stood precisely three inches tall. That's why he looked neither up nor down to anyone. Or thought he didn't.

But in Chuck's case, Tony felt he had to make an exception, just as he had for Fred Curtis. Nothing Chuck had done had altered Tony's first impression of him. Chuck was trained to say the right things, but they didn't sound right. Something about his eyes, too, had made Tony suspicious. Chuck had the eyes of a predator. Or a bigot, which to Tony was the same thing. When people were that narrow and small, you had to bend down real low and squint hard just to see them.

The look on Tony's face was hardly friendly, but Chuck was sure he knew where it was coming from.

"Hey, wait up, Tony." Chuck caught up with him a few feet from his office and put an arm around Tony's shoulders in as fraternal a gesture as possible, and he walked him a little further away from Martha's desk. Tony looked at him sourly.

"Hey, I understand, ole man. I mean, I'd be mad, too, being two-timed like that. And I mean like *that*." He almost sounded sincere; he certainly sounded fraternal. He lowered his voice and glanced at Martha, who was typing like a madwoman and ignoring them.

"Tell me, though, Tony. And you know you can tell *me*," Chuck's voice dripped. "Didn't you ever get 'em both? I mean, a guy like *you*. How could you pass up a three-way with *those* two?"

Tony just glared at him. From the look on Chuck's face, he was vicariously enjoying Tony's supposed exploits as much as his ultimate failure to convert Elizabeth. To what, Tony couldn't imagine. Catholic? "It's a shame, though, ole man. You know? What a waste. Both of them." Chuck hung his head and shook it sadly.

Tony's heart pulsed in his temples as if it had moved its headquarters. "The term *waste*," Tony hissed, ominously close to Chuck's nose, "implies that somehow something might have been available for your *use*." He took a breath and stared with cold lava eyes. "Elizabeth is *not* a *commodity* and she was *never available!*"

Chuck looked at him as if seeing him for the first time and stepped back slightly. He gripped Tony's shoulder in genuine concern. "You still love her, don't you?"

Tony moved closer and cupped Chuck's face in both hands, a vice-like grip. Chuck froze.

"Yeah. *Ole man*. I do." He stared at him one long second so his next words would hit right where he aimed. "Even more than the *man* I *slept* with last night."

The words pried Chuck's eyes a little wider and his mouth, but nothing else was working. He couldn't move. Down the hall he saw David leaning against Martha's desk, both watching the scene intently. Tony stepped back and with mock gentleness, almost maternally, removed Chuck's hand from his shoulder and held it in both of his, giving Chuck's wrist several sharp whacks.

"Watch where you put this, Gracie," Tony lisped exaggeratedly. Then he dropped his voice to his normal low register and bit Chuck with his eyes venomously. "I don't want anyone to think we're friends." He threw Chuck's hand at him and spun on his heel so precisely that even his old Marine DI would have been impressed. He closed his office door in Chuck's face with a quiet click.

* * *

The pounding on Elizabeth's door would not relent. Elizabeth wrapped her robe around her, still dripping from the tub, her hair in a towel turban.

"I swear, Kincaid," she said under her breath toward the owner of the insistent knuckles. "*Never* use your own keys." She jerked open the door without looking and without covering herself too well or being very aware of the wet T-shirt look her robe now had.

Then she saw it was not Kincaid at all and jumped slightly. Leaning against the doorframe and holding a large, half-empty highball glass, Chuck offered his best Robert Redford smile for her approval.

It wasn't approved or returned. Elizabeth pulled her robe around her as his eyes explored her, then the room beyond. Her eyes narrowed suspiciously.

"Aren't you going to invite me in? I, uh, didn't know when you'd be back on campus and I need those, uh, books I loaned you."

Elizabeth hesitated, then opened the door wider. Too late, she smelled the Scotch that hung around him like bad company as he moved past her and surveyed the room. He waved the glass in a long arc, indicating the furnishings. "Nice," he said. Only a slight slur was detectable. He took a long gulp from his glass.

"I'll get the books," she said flatly. She had stopped trying to understand this man. She just wanted him to leave with as little unpleasantness as possible.

He watched her walk out of the room toward the back of the house and couldn't help the partial erection beginning in his khakis. Preferred Elizabeth to help it. He turned toward the kitchen, still exploring, and saw the row of liquor bottles on a shelf. Looking at his near-empty tumbler, he reached for the Scotch and poured another half-glass, assessed the resultant color, and added another superfluous shot. He screwed the cap back on and turned to find Elizabeth watching him, his stack of books in her arms. She had put on a bulky terry robe over her wet one. The muscle in her jaw pulsed and she stared evenly at him.

He smiled even more winningly and raised his glass to her. "Hope you don't mind." He watched her over the rim of his glass as he took a long swallow. He liked it when women were put out with him, even angry. He thought it was amusing and added something to the challenge, something else to be changed, to be overcome. He took another gulp and thought about Tony. What a wimp, he thought. What a jerk-off.

Her impatience was changing to disgust, and she felt the change inside herself as she silently watched his face, hoping, knowing that surely he could read her eyes. He was looking at her, but not at her face, and she was going to knock him into the middle of next week if he didn't stop this eyeball groping. She turned toward the front door. He followed.

"I was hoping you could help me with some research." He made no attempt to mask the suggestive implication in his voice.

She turned toward him and held out the books. At best, he's tedious, she thought. About as much fun as watching cells divide. "Chuck . . . I don't want to be rude. But, then, why not? You are. I have plans this evening. And, lucky me, they do *not* include you."

He ignored the books, his eyes not stopping their roving over her body. "Only one car outside. Alone, aren't you?" He swallowed the rest of his drink and strained against the front of his pants. Surely, he thought, she can see it by now. "You're tense, Elizabeth. You need to relax . . . I think your problem is you've never had a real man."

Elizabeth drilled her eyes through Chuck's skull. "My *problem, son,*" she growled, "is your continued presence in my house." She spun on her heel and reached for the door, jerked it open and again extended the books toward him. "I suggest you leave before Kincaid gets home. It's late."

He shifted from one foot to the other; his eyes, somewhere deep in them, were almost hurt. He looked down at his feet and followed her to the door. She sighed, relieved.

But he leaned against the door frame and smiled again, this time not so charmingly, but hard, cold. "I think I'll just wait. *Watching* you two might be very . . . educational. For a while. But my talent's on the field, not in the stands." He pulled at his belt, readjusting himself slightly. God, look at those eyes; she's *furious* now, he thought.

That he had come here at all made her boil; that he had his arrogant, turgid self still here had her to the edge of the crater. But she held on to the rim, remembering her mother's constantly boring, thus calming tape that played uninvited in her head like the notes from some inane commercial jingle decrying waxy build-up. Consider the source, dear, her mother chanted in absentia. Which was where Chuck had better escort himself if he ever cared to see the dark side of thirty.

"Chuck," she said with icy contempt, "your *existence*, as far as I'm concerned, is superfluous. And your adolescent fantasies about me are *your* problem. I have neither the energy nor the inclination to help you grow up." She tossed his books out the open door. "Now. Get out."

She had sliced into him somehow, somewhere in a place he hadn't known existed. If he thought about it at all, what she'd said might stick with him, might make sense, might have some teeth in it or truth to it. And then he'd have to see how it fit into his life, and that would take forever. Pieces of truth insist on fitting; and in a tight, narrow mind there's seldom any extra space for anything new.

It was easier to reach up next to Elizabeth's head and slam the door behind her, pinning her to it with his body. He watched her face as he latched the door and lowered his mouth to hers. He could see no fear, only disgust and contempt and somewhere beyond that, pity.

He covered her mouth with his with as much tenderness as he could devise. She didn't move; she was like a pillow or an air mattress. Now when he looked at her, there was nothing but fury on her face. He covered her mouth again and forced his tongue between her teeth.

She clamped her jaws down like a shark. He howled and jumped away from her, checking his mouth for blood, a small trickle beginning down his jaw. He wiped it on his sleeve as she backed around the couch, watching him but looking for some kind of weapon.

The smile on his face had nothing in it but contempt for these pitiable attempts of hers. He knew his definition of the inevitable and that it was universal and absolute. He started toward her.

Jesus God, Kincaid, she screamed in her head, backing toward the palms and ferns. Get your skinny ass home. For *once* in your life, be on time.

She backed around the end of the couch, putting it between them, and she was closer to the door.

He knew that he had the advantage of size and speed, and he lunged toward the end of the couch to round it before she reached her escape.

She was at the door and fumbling with the latch in an instant, her hands not working right. And behind her she heard a dull thud, like a fist hitting soft flesh, and she heard something that sounded like a barbell falling noisily to the floor. She jerked the door open and glanced over her shoulder, and she saw Chuck frozen in pain at the end of the couch, and heard him explode in a rush of air escaping as a surprised, anguished groan. He bent double and grabbed his groin, all of his appendages suddenly helpless.

Poindexter, Elizabeth's cast iron canine sentinel, lay on the floor on his side, his silent, guilty snout still pointing toward his target in Chuck's hands. Poindexter had finally redeemed himself as guardian and protector, though the palms and ferns might have argued that point.

The blood in his face, the smile on his lips and the air in his lungs left Chuck as if by consensus. He clutched pointlessly at the expired membership between his legs, slowly folded like an out-of-date roadmap onto the floor, and sat staring dumbly at the rigid canine figure that had just crushed his manhood.

Outside, Elizabeth heard a car door shut, and Kincaid's castaneting high heels echoed up the walk. Kincaid, as usual, wasn't watching where she was going, tripped over one of the books on the sidewalk, and almost landed in Elizabeth's arms. She stopped and picked up the book, looking at it as if it had intentionally reached up and grabbed her leg, then at Elizabeth with at least as much accusation. Before she could get her mouth formed to ask whence cometh, she saw a strange but handsome man kneeling beyond the couch on their oriental carpet, his head bowed and his eyes closed in silent anguish.

She looked at Elizabeth and whispered, dead serious, "Who's he? Is he praying?" When Elizabeth started to laugh a moment later, Kincaid's confusion only grew. But Elizabeth laughed so hard, holding her sides and wiping her eyes that Kincaid started to laugh, too. The young man had apparently missed the punch line, for he didn't move, his strange religion still a mystery to Kincaid. Maybe he was friend of Mr. Falwell.

From behind a palm, Amelia peered with oblique little cat eyes at Poindexter's innocently guilty snout and minced over to this oddly immobile human male who had so recently been whipping around the room like her favorite fuzzy duck of prey. There was something about this man that smelled funny. Funny peculiar. She sniffed again and sneezed wetly all over his arm, twitched her nose disdainfully and strode archly away. People who wore that cologne were hopelessly bourgeois, often crass. She was allergic to it and them and usually didn't allow them in her home. Elizabeth, being a Democrat, didn't understand the intricacies of the class system nor how to use them. No doubt that was why she and Kincaid had the poor grace to be laughing at her still and again.

Chuck hauled himself to a Cro-Magnon stance and crept silently past Elizabeth and Kincaid, whose sputtering laugh died like a flooded engine. She stared at Elizabeth, then at Chuck as he inched past, still holding himself. She stared at where his hands were, her bewilderment complete. Kincaid still didn't want to seem rude and silently mouthed a question to Elizabeth.

"Who *is* he?"

Chuck stumbled over each book on his way out, only their position a concern to him now, not their content. Elizabeth slammed the door behind him and locked it, staring at the back of his head with X-ray vision.

"Bugbrain," she said to the sub-reptilian portion of his cranium.

* * *

His sounds filled the room. Sounds of passion and release and gratitude. No tenderness at this point, because he couldn't think at this point; his entire being existed in a few inches of flesh and the flesh around it. He had touched her and watched her eyes and said all that he had felt, and the words seemed true, the right things to say: She'd gone to bed with him. It had been quick like he liked it.

He couldn't tell if she'd liked it though. She didn't move much. Now he was suddenly so sleepy, he forgot that he was going to ask her. If it wasn't right, there would be other times. He'd get it.

Jake rolled off Lisa's nakedness and almost immediately started to snore softly. He hadn't seen the tears in her eyes, and she turned her head toward the wall and cried silently on his narrow dormitory bed. Outside, it began to rain again and in the distance she could see the lightning; but the thunder remained somewhere else and strangely silent.

A sob filled her throat and she pressed her hand to her mouth and glanced at Jake. He turned in his sleep but didn't wake.

Slowly she disentangled herself from him and the sheets and gently inched herself toward the end of the bed. She stood, feeling for her clothes, still crying silently, and began to button her shirt. As she picked up her jeans, something fell off the desk or out of her pocket and clanged around on the floor.

Jake stirred and put his arm around where she'd been on the bed. He turned over and sat up, rubbing his eyes, "Lisa?" He saw her in the light from under the door. "What are you doing?" he said groggily as he got out of bed.

She turned away from him, controlled her voice, and wiped her eyes. "Leaving."

He came up behind her, running his hands under her blouse and moving languidly against her roundness. "No you're not," he said gently. "We haven't finished yet. We've barely begun." He turned her around and lifted her blouse, then cupped her face as he pulled her to him. He felt her tears in his hands then, and he was stunned, aching for her, suddenly wanting to cradle her, comfort her.

"Oh, baby. I'm sorry. I hurt you. God, I'm sorry." Oh God, how could he fix it? It was done and she hurt and how could he fix it? His arms and chest ached with wanting to comfort her and wanting her to comfort him. If her tears didn't stop, he was afraid his would start.

"You didn't hurt me, Jake" she said softly. "It's not that. It's not you. It's me. I just want to go." She turned from him and pulled on her jeans.

"But what did I do?" he pleaded. "What, Lisa?" He was getting frustrated. How could he fix it if she wouldn't talk to him?

But she had nothing to say. It was like she was hearing a song in a foreign language in her head, and she hadn't translated the words into her own tongue yet, much less his. He sighed heavily.

"Look, Lisa. My roommate said I could have the room anytime I wanted it. When can I see you again?"

She didn't answer. She picked up her purse and felt for her keys.

"Wednesday?" he asked.

"No."

"Then when?" His voice rose an octave.

Tears still pouring down her face, she looked at him sadly, wordlessly and closed the door behind her, leaving his question, among other things, dangling.

She heard his door open as she walked down the hall toward the side exit. "I can't read your goddamn mind, Lisa!" he shouted at her back. She pushed on the door under the red four-letter word, and rain began to wash the salt from her face.

She climbed in her car and sat crying for a long while. Finally she started the car and sped out onto the street, then to the freeway, the storm outside now equal to the one within her. She could barely see through either torrent, her wipers only a little more efficient than her sleeves.

She listed to the right, into someone else's space. A blast like ten horns of Gabriel filled her head, and an eighteen-wheeler roared by just beyond the paint on her right rear fender. She clutched the wheel, her knuckles white, her breath nonexistent, and whipped back toward another lane as the tailgate flashed by. Somehow, before the truck blocked her view, she saw a big green overhead sign, and the name of a street registered in her brain. Her hands now on automatic pilot, she swerved across a lane toward the exit.

She couldn't see the other fists being shaken at her or the voices raised in the collisions that almost occurred, the adrenalin that pumped without utility all over the highway. Now the rain poured as if the Lord had an announcement to make; crushing thunder, blinding lightning arrived together as if for the end of another world. She felt it might be hers.

* * *

The pounding on Elizabeth's front door would not relent. Finally she pulled on her robe and looked hesitantly at the door from a safe distance.

Kincaid stood behind her in the hallway door gripping an old sorority paddle in her hand. It was made of solid walnut and would crack open any blinking noggin that came through that door. Kincaid was not above raw, bloody violence. Not where Chuck Gardner was concerned. If that arrogant amalgamation of bacteria was back at that door, Elizabeth was supposed to let him in and lure him to the hall. Then Kincaid would dispatch him to the land of Nod via her walnut mystic goody, a gift from her beloved Grecian sisters. *Then* call the police.

She nodded at Elizabeth and widened her stance, the weight of the paddle, really a carved one-by-four, resting in her other hand. Martina Navratilova could not have returned the serve she was prepared to deliver.

Elizabeth crept to the door and peeked through the peephole. And without any hesitation, hastily in fact, she threw off the bolt and jerked the door open.

Lisa stood soaking wet and heaving huge sobs in the pouring rain. She saw Elizabeth and crumpled into her arms, gasping for breath only to lose it again in the next wave. Elizabeth knew the only thing she could do was hold her, so she put her arms around this soaked bundle of old faded jeans and rocked her, stroking her hair and cooing useless maternalisms softly.

Kincaid took one look and opted for a discreet retreat, knowing her presence would be awkward if not altogether redundant.

Finally Lisa quieted, like the waves from a ship that crash on the shore then slowly blend back into the rhythm of the sea herself. She pulled away from Elizabeth and wiped her eyes, still gasping but not so desperate.

"I'm sorry. I know it's late. I don't even know how I ended up here."

"That's all right, Lisa. Come here and sit down. It's terrible out there," she said gently as thunder rolled around the earth.

Lisa sank exhaustedly into the couch and looked tentatively at Elizabeth. "Could I have some wine or something?"

Elizabeth hesitated a moment. She couldn't let her drive for a while anyway. "Sure. Ok. You wait there." She came back from the kitchen with a glass of wine and a large towel. Lisa took them from her as Elizabeth sat next to her, her hand trembling, and gulped down half the glass before Elizabeth could stop her.

She touched Lisa's hand and pulled the glass gently away. "Hey. Slow down there."

Lisa lowered the glass and looked shakily at her hands as she wrapped them around the glass. Elizabeth took her towel and pressed it around Lisa's shoulders and wiped rain off Lisa's cheek with her palm. Lisa shivered involuntarily and took another shaky gulp of wine.

Elizabeth didn't know what had sent Lisa here but she thought she knew why; somehow, intuitively, she knew why.

Lisa gulped the wine again and sat in the humid silence, expecting something from Elizabeth, but not knowing what. And Elizabeth looked so tired. Lisa suddenly felt out of place, lost. "Look. I'll go. You want me to go."

Elizabeth shook her head gently and put her hand on Lisa's shoulder and wouldn't let her stand. "I don't want you to leave, Lisa. I want you to talk to me."

Elizabeth's hand seared into Lisa's shoulder, and Lisa looked at her, her eyes pleading for something that had no name. She felt transparent and looked away. "Is is true . . .? What the papers said?" Lisa almost whispered.

"Yes," Elizabeth answered softly. The two of them might as well have been in church.

"But . . . you *can't* be. I've seen *queers* . . . *dykes* . . . You're not *like* them."

"I *am* them, Lisa," she said, her voice soft as velvet. "Is that why you came here? To ask me that?"

Lisa scoured Elizabeth's face again. *Was* that why? *Was* it? "I don't know . . . I don't know." Her hands were trembling, her voice even more. And here was this woman in her goddamn robe and nothing else, and I'm getting her goddamn furniture wet, and I look like death warmed over eating a Triscuit. *Wine*? Why the hell didn't I ask for some Drāno? "Oh, Jesus. I don't know *anything* anymore. My whole life's just—" Her voice trailed off. "I . . . went to bed with Jake tonight." Tears welled up in her eyes again, and the wine sloshed precariously in her hand. "*Stupid*. Trying to prove something."

"To yourself?" The therapist wouldn't leave.

"Yes."

"Did you?"

When Lisa answered, she hardly had any air left. Elizabeth's perfume filled the room and she could hardly breathe; Elizabeth filled her lungs. It was that same perfume. Oh, god. Nita had worn that same perfume. "No," she answered in a whisper. "It's not his fault. It's me." She glanced quickly at Elizabeth, knowing how she always looked at her when she had said that in her therapy sessions. The look was there. "Well, it *is* me! It *is* my fault!" Lisa pleaded for an answer, some relief, with her eyes. "I *know* what love feels like. And it's not like that. Not with him."

"With who, then?"

Lisa was breathing as if she had run a long, long way and hadn't hit her stride. Her hands shook uncontrollably. Elizabeth leaned forward and took the glass from her and set it on the table in front of them, realizing too late that her face was only inches from Lisa's. Lisa looked up at her, searching Elizabeth's eyes, the question still ringing in her ears, and moved her lips across the abyss to the soft, full answer of Elizabeth's mouth. That mouth. Those lips. Under hers. Inside hers.

Something within Lisa wrenched at her, twisted in her, and her arms went weak, the bones all liquid in her legs as she seemed to be melting into Elizabeth, drowning and wanting to, holding absolutely still. She felt Elizabeth's soft, warm breath against her cheeks. Then her even softer fingers there, not pulling toward and not pushing away.

Lisa leaned back slightly, looked into Elizabeth's eyes and waited, asking yet not knowing what to ask, her heart thundering with the storm outside.

Elizabeth raised her other hand to Lisa's face, gently kissed her forehead as if putting a child to sleep and pulled Lisa's head toward her to rest on her shoulder, rocking her slowly, slowly in tiny, rhythmic movements like the ocean when the tide's in.

After an eon, Lisa's breathing slowed and she settled against Elizabeth, exhausted now and not wanting anything but this soothing motion of comfort and sleep. She knew Elizabeth wasn't her answer, had wanted her to be, but knew she wasn't. And was glad, relieved that Elizabeth knew it before she did, that there was neither expectation nor rejection in the way Elizabeth held her, only a warm, protected space.

Nita had had a warm space for her, too; but Nita had taken it away, sealed it shut.

The only other person Lisa has ever felt this way with had been Nita. She had kissed Nita once like that, and Nita had returned it so unexpectedly, so voraciously, that it had scared them both. But it frightened Nita more. And now Lisa couldn't talk to her, didn't know what Nita felt then or was feeling now, didn't know what anyone was feeling, didn't know what she felt herself.

Elizabeth looked at the small figure in her arms, breathing rythmically now. And her arms hurt; she felt like crying. It was like holding herself when she was younger. How can we ever make it easier for someone else, she thought. Except to make them know they're not alone.

Elizabeth gazed over Lisa's head at the still, coral coals of the fire, her eyes distant, her voice in another time, another place, remembering something painfully important, a thread, a guide wire for herself at least, maybe even for Lisa.

"I had a friend once in college. My best friend. Beautiful girl . . . woman. We made each other laugh . . . and cry. When we weren't together, we were on the phone planning to be together. Even made sure our boyfriends got along so we could go to dances and movies together."

Lisa pulled slowly away and watched Elizabeth, hearing the story as if hearing her own voice. There was a volume on Lisa's face, and Elizabeth read it well.

She smiled sadly at Lisa because she knew the end of both stories, had heard it a million times in her sleep and in Lisa's eyes, in Kincaid's, the Lord knew who else. She stood and walked to the fireplace, watching Lisa's image in the mirror, her voice still soft, distant.

"But there was something else between my best friend and me. We didn't talk about it. She didn't want to name what we felt. Neither did I. We used words like 'sisters.' Oh, and 'maternal.' " She laughed sadly. "Maternal. That's the best one." She looked back in the mirror. The distance between them was only time and perception, framed in glass the same, held in feelings the same.

"Whenever she hurt . . . bad grades . . . her boyfriend . . . anything . . . she'd come to me. I knew her better than *anyone* knew her."

"Nita," Lisa whispered to herself. "Like Nita and me." She looked up at Elizabeth's reflection, then her own, then Elizabeth's eyes on hers as Elizabeth spoke.

"Then I made the mistake of telling her I loved her. What we both already knew, both already felt. As if anyone could possibly have missed it in our eyes when we looked at each other." She closed her eyes with the weight of remembering it and let out a breath that seemed to have been in her for years, sadness that didn't go away but hid, aging in a child's game. "I don't know what happened then. I called. She didn't. She was cold. I was frozen. I heard she got married that summer." She made a small ironic little noise. "I wasn't *Gay* then. I was destroyed."

Lisa blinked, as if she'd been watching a foreign film and had seen her name in the credits. She wanted to cry again or hold Elizabeth or hold herself. She felt as though she'd been swimming forever and had finally brushed the sandy bottom with her toes. Elizabeth turned around. Lisa stumbled toward something to say.

"You must have felt so . . . I guess there was no one to talk to then, no one to . . . You must have felt so . . . alone . . . different. . . ." Now Lisa's gaze went inward. "Numb . . . felt numb inside. Alone . . . it couldn't be . . . not what they said . . . not like *that*. . . . I just loved *Nita*, that's all. Just Nita . . . just her . . ."

The focus changed and Lisa saw herself in the mirror, watched herself looking back, then Elizabeth's intense dark eyes, watchful like a mother's with a child on a balance beam. Slowly, tentatively, Lisa touched her own lips, remembering a kiss. Perhaps tonight's. Perhaps not. "How can love be wrong? How *can* it be?"

Lisa had stepped off the beam and was on the ground and Elizabeth smiled.

"The right question *is* helpful, isn't it?" Elizabeth said.

And Lisa began to smile, too, hurting still, but not as much and still confused, but not alone, blind and wounded. She felt suddenly incredibly peaceful, like she had walked a hundred miles and finally had been allowed to sit down and might even be allowed to sleep.

Elizabeth walked to the hallway door and peered around it. Kincaid gasped, shot up into the air and clutched at her heart. "Don't *do* that, Elizabeth! God, I'm having a stroke!"

Elizabeth grinned. "You can come out now, Mother Phillips. We need a chef, dear. Not a chaperone." And to Lisa, "You hungry?"

* * *

Jake's concentration on the field was usually his strongest suit. No matter how rowdy the crowd, how bloodthirsty the defensive line, his eyes and his being followed the ball as if he procreated with it. It was this, more than raw talent, though that was adequate, which made him shine and which made him the custodian of his coach's future.

Today's practice was of such a caliber that Coach Crutcher was sure that what his own future held was the promise of a janitorial position in Greenland. And soon. Jake, Crutcher's salvation, had all the concentration today of a hydrangea bush who was in the process of choosing to be blue rather than pink.

Jake straggled into the locker room behind his teammates, men who had looked to him for direction and spark and found mumbled signals and broken plays. Nothing was going right for Jake, and all he wanted was a cold beer and a little piece and quiet. That's how he spelled it, and that's what he meant.

He peeled off his sweaty jersey and drug himself toward his locker wanting just to melt into the walls, hoping no one would speak to him. The only thing that made him feel worth anything was this game, and today he wasn't worth shit. All he could think about was Lisa, round and round with no end to it, no answer.

Scooter popped him on the butt with a rolled towel and grinned at him. "Come on, Jake. It's no big deal. Coach is hard on everybody. He'd find something wrong with an eighty yard field goal."

Jake just shook his head silently and tugged at his shoes. His arms hurt so bad he could hardly move.

The locker room was always noisy after practice, celebrating a good one or dissecting a bad one. But now, from near the door, a silence began to spread like a cancer and all of them knew who had come in the room. Eyes turned and mouths closed as Coach Crutcher swaggered between the benches.

"Splendid practice, girls!" he bellowed. "Just splendid." He slapped each player with his eyes as he passed them. "Never seen such a graceful troop of ballerinas *in my life*." He slapped his clipboard against his thigh and rocked on the balls of his feet, looking from one downcast face to another. Then his eyes perched on Jake like a vulture.

"And if it isn't Isadora herself," Coach sneered. Behind him he heard a few snickers and whirled on them, hurling javelin eyes, stopping them in mid-snick. He stalked over to Jake and lowered his voice slightly as he pulled out a pink sheet of paper from his clipboard and shoved it toward Jake. "I can't throw the ball for you, Tyler. And I can't take your exams." He glared around at his other players who had stopped undressing and were watching Jake. "You people enjoying this show? 'Cause if you are, I'd be *real* pleased to audition *your* ass next."

He glared at them a moment until not a single eye remained on him, then turned back toward Jake. "I want you to tell me how you expect to play ball here if you're not *enrolled*?" He shook the pink sheet at him again. "Are you *trying* to flunk out?"

Jake looked helpless and bewildered. "No, Coach, I—"

"Biology: *D-minus*," Crutcher interrupted, reading from the pink sheet. "American History: *F*."

Jake snatched the sheet from in front of his face and stared at it as if it had been a document tracing his lineage to Sri Lanka. Inside him the fury grew until it pushed at the walls of his heart and his brain.

* * *

There was an animal in his head, a small, rabid, vicious, wounded animal that clawed at his eyes and rampaged around between his ears screaming and devouring all logic in its path. Jake held his head in his hand, the headache thundering in his temples. Lisa's voice over the phone was making no sense at all.

"I don't understand, Lisa. Why won't you see me?" She may as well have been speaking French. "Shit, Lisa. I *know* it's 'just you.' It sure as hell isn't *me*. Jesus. If you'd just talk to me. Tell me what I've—" He looked up as if a ghost had tapped him on the shoulder, his face suddenly ashen, cold. "What are you *talking* about? What are you talking about?" he pleaded. "You *can't* be, Lisa . . . What the hell's Nita got to do with anything?"

Every sphincter muscle he had clanged shut. The animal raged louder; having consumed logic, it lunged now toward a softer spot on the other side of Jake's head. He had lost everything and someone was going to pay, someone who had caused it all. If he could just figure out who that someone was.

* * *

It was midnight and past Dog's bedtime.

In the corner of the study, Dog lay with her chin resting on Dr. Harrison's foot, just the smallest pink tip of Dog's tongue sticking out from between her teeth. She watched the woman above her pondering the intricacies and absurdities of time between two more wars and was thankful the Lord had made her four-legged and fuzzy. Telepathy was a large help also, but hands would have been nice. Humans had probably invented doorknobs just to make a dog's life difficult by requiring that she concern herself with complicated things like Daylight Savings Time and consistent bladders. Daylight Savings Time had ruined her whole day and many a carpet.

Suddenly Dog tensed and focused her ears as she shot an angry look toward the front of the house, and she growled deep in her throat. She might be little and fuzzy and cute, but she could suck leg with the best of them.

"What is it, girl?" Dr. Harrison's eyes followed the direction of Dog's ears. Dog cocked one ear toward Dr. Harrison, then stood and growled louder.

Then Dr. Harrison heard it. A hissing sound, like the air being let out of a snake, scraping and bumping, a body in the bushes outside. She opened her desk drawer and pulled out the pearl-handled handgun her father had given her a thousand years ago. She walked quietly to the front door, saw that it was locked and bolted and flipped on the floodlight in her front yard. She pulled her curtain open an inch and saw Jake Tyler stumbling somewhat drunkenly across her yard in a large hurry. She didn't think he'd come to visit, not unless he had intended to repaint her wicker porch chairs for her, because in his hand was a can of Rusto Day-Glo Red. That seemed a rather garish and low rent choice of colors to her, so she supposed she should be thankful for small favors.

Then she saw it, saw his purpose not three inches from her nose, the glowing scarlet lines bleeding down the panes of glass in front of her, all across the front of her home. As if from the far side of a mirror, the huge red word took shape in her mind and screamed in blazing, searing tongues.

DYKE.

And bleeding down her face, the tears began to stream.

* * *

Geoffrey Meade sat in the presidential office silently reviewing his troops. Paul Thompson, a general and thus removed from the clutching, sharp stench of the fray, blustered at the failings of those of lesser rank, having as he did his world view, his ubiquitous Big Picture. But he was doing everything short of leaving the country to distance himself from both Fred Curtis and the horse Fred rode in on.

Sam Fitzhugh was doing the same thing but thought his distance was actual, being as he was a link in a separate chain of command. He satteth on the left hand of Meade, while Thompson levitated above and slightly to Meade's right on the official organizational chart.

Fred, as usual, sat with his ass in the middle and in a crack, trying to enlist or draft someone for support. Draft dodgers for this war surrounded him like debris in a cyclone.

"That's *ridiculous*, Curtis! *I* didn't stop you from raising those people's salaries!" Thompson rasped coldly. Now he knew why his secretary called Curtis "Old Thud and Blunder." Although he couldn't stand the man himself, he had dismissed the dishonorific as bitter, empty, female vengeance, his secretary siding with other clerical people that Curtis had handled. The man was hell on clerical people. Always had been. It was the only thing Thompson liked about him. Getting a raise or promotion out of Curtis was like extracting impacted twelve year molars. Right now Thompson heard the whining scream of a drill bit in his head, and his teeth ached from the clamp he had them in. "You didn't even discuss this with me! Curtis, you're on your own on this one, son," he lashed, blizzard air almost whipping out of his icy blue eyes and whirling around Curtis' spine til he shivered. "I don't care how many markers you think you can call in, boy, you're on your own on this one."

Curtis was tenacious if nothing else; he never deserted a ship, especially his own, although at present his dinghy was full of holes in a high sea. He bailed again and shifted pronouns. "They should've fired her years ago. Uppity bitch. A *dyke*, fachrissake!"

Fitzhugh glanced at Curtis. "If you *knew* that, Fred, why didn't *you* fire her."

"I *didn't* know." Curtis unthinkingly changed his story. Again. And just as quickly reversed his course. "That is, well, that is, I suspected, but not until—"

"That's hardly legal, is it, Sam?" Meade interrupted, his voice quiet, impatient, ominous.

Fitzhugh rocked his splayed palm in the air and twisted his mouth into a subjunctive line. "Risky," he said, then sliced his eyes toward Curtis. "In the *past* we've been careful not to *specify* that reason when we terminated those people." He had no written record of his meeting with Curtis, only that Curtis had been there. And as Fitzhugh had rewritten his version of their conversation, he had been very explicit in reminding Fred of the letter of the law. It wasn't his job to enforce it, only read it. Enforcement was somebody else's job, someone who reported through several people to Paul Thompson.

When he looked back at Meade, the man was looking at him as if somehow he held Fitzhugh responsible for Curtis' ineptitude. He was baffled and a little affronted. Meade looked back at Curtis, who shifted anxiously in his seat.

"This student you keep talking about," Meade said so quietly Fred had to lean forward to hear. "Hunter? Is that her name?" Curtis nodded, watching the president with the eyes of a dog about to be whipped, the error of his ways seeping toward his hind leg. Meade watched his eyes as if Fred's brain flashed cryptic messages out his baby browns and Meade had cracked the code.

"We seem to have a number of curious points in this story about some notes on Ms. Hunter. Dr. Gardner said you gave the notes to him. You say your secretary, Martha Huddleston, gave them to you, that Dr. McKay asked her to type them up, and that she then became concerned about their content. Ms. Huddleston said she's never seen any notes on anybody. Dr. McKay said they were . . . *pilfered* was the word she used. All I know is that everyone is belly deep in scraps of incriminating paper, and I've yet to lay eyes on them. Let me *see* the damn things, Curtis."

Curtis swallowed hard. "I don't have . . . that is, I didn't keep . . . that is, I could tell you the *gist* —"

Meade's eyes cut him short more terminally than any barked command could have. "Your *job*, Curtis, is the welfare of students. And you were willing to ruin the good name of one of them on the basis of documents not important enough to *keep*?" He was furious and at the same time was astonished, amazed at such tenacity for the untenable. It was increasingly clear from everything he'd investigated that Curtis' primary objective was to clothe his shiningly naked behind. For all its intricacies of application, C.Y.O.A. might as well be an advanced degree program.

With his eyes, Meade nailed Fitzhugh to his chair. Fitzhugh knew he was clean, so he was sure the anger he saw was left over from Curtis.

"This Hunter girl," Meade asked him. "She isn't mentioned in the suit, is she?" Fitzhugh shook his head. "Then I suggest none of you mention her either. Not again, not ever."

Fitzhugh shifted in his seat casually, feeling connected to Meade, on his team, on the winning side. "Look, Geoff. I know it looks bad, but since they didn't mention the girl, we might get McKay to drop the black-mail part. She wants the girl protected. Or so she says."

Meade's eyes narrowed. "I don't think you heard me, Sam. *I* want the girl protected."

A bead of sweat popped out on Fitzhugh's upper lip, and he could feel his armpits steam.

"Right. Well. Yes. Then as far as the salary part of it: That, we can handle." Fitzhugh sought fraternity in the president's eyes, and finding none, looked for kinships through further explanation. "In salary cases, the institution always has the edge if we go through appeals. Once we get through the first trial, we drag it out as long as it'll stretch. Wear the McKay woman down. Her resources can't outlast ours."

Now Meade not only looked impatient, but almost disgusted, hostile. But Fitzhugh missed his expression because he had glanced at Thompson and smiled a conspirator's smile. "Haven't lost a discrimination case yet," he said proudly.

"Have we been guilty?" Meade asked quietly.

Fitzhugh looked from Thompson back to his own meticulously manicured cuticles, still smiling. "I only said we hadn't *lost*," he said jovially, missing entirely the significance of Meade's ominously quiet voice. Then Fitzhugh looked up at his boss and a great, invisible, darkly feathered bird flew over his head, reached down and peeled the smile from his face. This was a new game under a new captain, though the rules had been around long enough to collect dust and cobwebs, these rules having lain around rather idle.

"How much is she asking for?" Meade asked.

"Too much," said Fitzhugh. He wasn't slow, just rusty. He read the last rule in Meade's even stare, and kicked himself. He sighed, not really liking this game; in this one, there were no secretly coded signals, no fancy footwork, no head fakes. He preferred intrigue and maneuvering. He reached in his brief-case, pulled out a sheet of paper with figures on it and handed it to Meade.

"We could try for a out-of-court, Geoff. I've talked to her lawyer, though. I don't know. Her lawyer, or *whatever* she is, is a cold bitch. Won't budge an inch so far." Fitzhugh thought about the Phillips woman and clucked to himself over the waste of it all. And over the wrench this woman threw in the gears of his style. Right in the middle of his argument, he'd look up and find her in a dazzling smile with those eyes of hers locked somewhere below his belt, and he'd begin to stammer like an aphasiac.

Meade looked at the sheet of figures a moment, then at each of the men in front of him. Slowly, he pushed his chair back, stood and walked to the massive window that framed his campus. He stood there, arms folded across his chest, saying nothing, his back to the three of them.

He had come back to his Alma Mater after thirty years and two presidencies at other schools, and it had felt like coming home. He loved this place, every brick, every book. They were one and the same: this school, his career, his soul. It seemed incredible to him that in a collective endeavor supposedly dedicated to growth and learning and integrity, that this sort of thing could go on. He wasn't naive, but it astounded him every time he found it, found someone with the incredible blindness of looking outward but never in, of not having the good sense to reach toward the excellence their motto said was their goal. He laughed to himself. Of course they all *said* they *strove* for excellence and integrity. Who the hell would chisel above a Gothic arch that they would *strive* for mediocrity and deceit.

The silence grew in length and depth until even Paul Thompson began to squirm and to be a little concerned about the creatures who might lurk below these murky waters, and he shifted again in his seat. Fitzhugh, out of the corner of his eye, saw Thompson's lip twitch and saw him wipe his palms on his trousers. Fitzhugh had never before seen Thompson sweat, even on the golf course. He had thought perhaps the man had somehow healed himself of the bothersome necessity of excreting anything.

Curtis didn't move, could hear everyone breathing as if they'd all been locked in the dark hold of an old damp ship. Had there been any way for him to pull it off unmolested, he would have crept out of the room while Meade was still turned away.

He was halfway considering it, when he saw Meade's head begin to revolve toward him. What Curtis saw in his face was more justice than mercy. Meade pierced each man with a separate, individually sharpened stare, before he spoke in those same dangerously quiet tones.

"When I was in school here, gentlemen, I learned a lot of things. One of them was how to make a decision with some sense of honor. I ask myself three questions about each option available: Is it right? Is it legal? And is it fair? If my choice gets a 'no' on any of them, there's something wrong. Either with my decision or the system that allowed me to make it."

He looked at Curtis with contempt. "You apparently didn't even bother to ask the questions." Then he looked at Thompson. "And it was your job to make sure he had." Then at Fitzhugh. "And yours: to *tell* them the questions if they didn't already know them. *And* the answers, if those escaped them as well."

He walked to his bookcase and pulled out a bound, thick paperback that looked like a small phone book, walked to Thompson and handed it to him. "This is our personnel policy, Paul. Use it. And make sure your people use it."

Fitzhugh was enjoying this so much, he forgot he might be next. No one alive, as far as he knew, had ever told Paul Thompson what to do and survived unscathed. But Meade would; he wouldn't be touched, he could tell by Thompson's speechless, dejected eyes. Fitzhugh's euphoria at witnessing the end of a reign was short lived. Meade turned his piercing eyes on him in the next instant.

"I want this thing settled, Sam. Out of court. I want it done right, and I want it done now." Fitzhugh nodded solemnly once. He was afraid any more than one nod would be wasting Meade's time.

"How long have you been here, Curtis?" Now it was Fred's turn, and he screwed his twitching, shining cheeks into his chair.

"Seventeen years," he said weakly, his voice cracking slightly, as though thrashing anew under the onslaught of puberty.

"I suggest you update your resumé. Indicate your resignation date to be the last day of this month."

Fred gasped. He had not been ready for this at all, didn't understand any of it. Why settle out of court, why give her anything at all? He couldn't believe what he was hearing. *He* didn't make the woman a queer, still didn't believe she really was one, not deep down. It was all moving too fast for someone who so steadfastly believed in his own innocence, and believed it in the face of all evidence to the contrary. Fred sputtered, near hysteria, "But . . . but . . . that's . . . that's not fair. . . ."

Smoothing his hair, Meade seemed to consider that statement for a moment, weigh it with his eyes. Fred sank in his chair, relieved, certain of a reprieve.

"You're right, Curtis. You're fired."

* * *

It was now ten minutes after the hour, and although they had heard the rumors, the class couldn't be certain until Dr. Harrison failed to show up altogether. Someone had heard she'd been late for two classes so far today and missed a third, that she was in the hospital with a stroke, that she'd skipped and gone to Tijuana and set up a used hurachi shop.

The stories about Dr. Harrison's unusual behavior today had left the realm of sanity and were mere diversion by the time this graduate seminar met. One of the men watched the time until he could legally leave, due deference for Dr. Harrison defined to the second, the respect allotted to a full professor being twenty minutes. Over the last thirty years, having never drawn on this account, one would think she'd have accrued an additional minute or so, but no. Like annual leave and sick days, like muscle tone and summer peaches: Use it or lose it.

It was minus one minute and counting to freedom, when the young man looked toward the hall to see Dr. Harrison moving slowly through the door, her head bowed. She closed the door behind her and drifted to her seat. She seemed to have sent her body for a proxy vote in whatever contest might be scheduled for today, because her eyes and the mind they revealed hadn't yet arrived.

Her students became immediately silent when they saw her, as they always did, but they looked at each other, now concerned that she was indeed sick, that the hospital story might be close to the truth. They had never seen her move so ponderously, as though her slim body hid a growth of some kind. And she suddenly seemed old, actually old, and it had never occurred to them before to consider that measure of her, because they hadn't thought of her as so different from themselves since her mind was so like theirs.

She sat in her usual seat and still she neither looked at anyone nor spoke, her eyes focusing somewhere beyond their heads. They shifted in the silence, primitives witnessing an eclipse, something new and frightening, without ceremony or ritual to control its meaning or occurrence.

A young woman stacked and restacked her notes, watching her professor more intently than the others, waiting. Finally, she cleared her throat and said tentatively, "Dr. Harrison . . . would you like for me to begin? Or . . . do you . . . prefer to make your usual opening remarks?"

In slow motion, Dr. Harrison looked toward the woman speaking to her, her eyes finally bringing the face and the words into focus. The answer jumped from side to side in front of her, and annoyed by the motion, she batted it toward the woman with one hand. "Yes, yes. Do I have to spoon feed you people?" Her voice startled even its owner with its unexpected harshness, and the young woman blinked and swallowed as much of her hesitation as would fit down her throat. Everyone glanced from the professor to the woman, then drilled their concentration into the table around which they sat.

The woman rose and carried her papers to the podium. Behind her on the blackboard was a long quotation that she'd written there before class, no doubt critical to the point she intended to make in her presentation. She knew though that some of her colleagues felt it their unerring duty to miss or prevent any point she claimed for herself. Score or be scored upon. So she steeled herself for the drive and began.

"Let's begin today's discussion of Hitler and his rise to power by examining the social climate in Germany following World War I."

Dr. Harrison slipped back into herself, not listening to anything around her, not seeing, not thinking really, not with constructs or paradigms or theorems, but images flashing behind her eyes, things mostly crimson, amber, vivid mist.

There was a commotion rampaging somewhere outside her head, and her name was being called. Slowly Dr. Harrison looked from one student's face to another all of whom for some reason had nominated her as the center of their circumference.

"Your conclusions are trite, hardly anything approaching revelation," the clock watcher complained to the young woman at the podium.

"My *point*," she jousted causticly, "is that America is the Germany of the 80's. The parallels are legion. Or is your purpose in studying history merely to *record* events as opposed to *learn* from them?"

He turned disgustedly to Dr. Harrison who seemed to be ignoring him and sought her support again. "You're the expert on this, Dr. Harrison. What do you think?"

She looked at him as though he were a stranger and she herself afflicted with amnesia. Outside, the bell was ringing and the students watched her as they stacked their books, beginning not to expect their referee to rule and deciding the penalty would have to wait until the real Dr. Harrison could be found to depose this pretender.

But the woman at the podium didn't move, afraid to leave Dr. Harrison alone but afraid to intrude. Someone must have died in her family or something, or she'd been told she had some disease. Beyond her head the chalked lines of words snaked in an incoherent, unrhythmic cotillion, squirming their way into Dr. Harrison's consciousness, until finally she saw them and began to read, her lips barely moving, no sound at all emerging.

In Nazi Germany *Seen the quote a thousand times, knew it by heart* . . . they first came for the communists and I didn't speak up because I wasn't a communist . . . *wasn't like them* . . . Then they came for the Jews, and I didn't speak up . . . *wasn't like* . . . because I wasn't a Jew; then they came for the . . . *wasn't like* . . . Catholics and I was a Protestant . . . And then . . . *wasn't* . . . they came for . . . *not like* . . . me and there was no one left to speak up . . . *like me.*

Jeanette sat rock still, somehow breathing, barely breathing, until the words floated free in her head and then settled, hardening in layer on layer like sediment becoming stone.

* * *

The sun had set, sucking color and light from the sky, and Jeanette sat in her study, phone in hand. The mass inside her was almost gone and with it the dank, musty air. She drummed her fingers on her open volume of Millay and touched the photograph marker resting next to it.

"Yes, officer, I'd like to report a case of vandalism. Well, yes, I can describe the culprit, but I think it might be more efficient to simply give you his name and address." She smiled at the Rusto can in a plastic bag on her desk. She rarely watched television, but that Perry Mason rerun had finally come in handy. She knew all about fingerprints and that Jake's were all over this can.

* * *

Elizabeth knew that life wasn't ever going to be cooperative enough to provide anything as satisfying as a conclusion, that unfinished business and loose ends were things to be endured like death itself; death being the most significant piece of unfinished business available to anyone, the ultimate subjunctive mood. She didn't really feel bad about what had happened to Fred in all this, she just felt unfinished somehow, that maybe if she'd liked him enough to talk to him, some of this could have been avoided. Kincaid reminded her that he hadn't given her much reason to like him.

"But that's like faith for sinners. The people that need it the most don't ask for it and rarely get it," Elizabeth had said. "And certainly don't deserve it." It wasn't that Kincaid didn't believe in heaven, she just thought that justice here on earth was so much more instructive to those individuals most in need of an education. The living resisted instruction by whatever means available, and the dead seemed beyond remediation.

For his part, in what seemed to Fred Curtis a conclusion, at least for him, he had returned to campus in the middle of the night, packed his things and departed, leaving no sign that he had ever been there. But just in case anyone remembered him, he made sure that no one at his former place of employment thought that he might be pining away for them. He leaked the information back in a gush that he would soon be selling sports equipment for his brother-in-law. And expected to make a killing.

That was exactly what Tony said he was going to make if Chuck opened his mouth by so much as a millimeter. Which didn't seem likely since Tony had been named acting head of the Center the day that Curtis left. And his first official act, since Elizabeth had told Tony of Chuck's charming attempt at romance, was to inform Chuck that he could either clean up his act or take it on the road. Chuck responded by Xeroxing twenty copies of his resumé and hiding in his office. Martha managed to type Chuck's letters of inquiry with amazing dispatch, smiling all the while as she personally stamped each one. Even used her own stamps.

Kincaid loved loose ends to tie and thought the only ones left were the ones for whose twining she had charge. But when she and Elizabeth arrived for the battle, she found that the enemy had surrendered last week. All her out-flanking and big guns lay cold and unconsumated on unopened yellow pads. What satisfaction was there in fighting with someone who said you were right? Well, there *was* a little bit: the look on Fitzhugh's face. He looked as though he were passing a kidney stone with each sentence of the conciliation agreement he read.

When they left the meeting Elizabeth was just relieved it was over, so they could rest up before the next crisis. She wanted to stay at the University; that commitment hadn't changed. She'd just have to wait and see if she could still be effective after all the uproar. Martha said she had already gotten more new requests for Elizabeth's time than she could schedule. But Elizabeth wasn't sure yet that she wanted to be counted as the official representative of another minority. She didn't know how "her people felt" on this or that issue and didn't know how to get in touch with many of them to ask. She only knew how *she* felt, which was exactly how she'd felt a month ago. Well, not exactly, but close enough. She felt like Elizabeth.

She smiled more now, and there had been one thing that had made her smile to her toes. Tony had called her Sunday morning to tell her who he'd met in the bar the night before. He was forever doing this, but this morning his voice sounded like a little boy with the prize egg on Easter morning. Last night he'd seen Fred Curtis' oldest son wrapped around the University's star wide receiver like a grape vine in ivy. Tony had introduced himself to them and explained who he was and how he knew who they were. After a small display of hysterics on Scooter's part, not to mention Fred Junior's, they all got over themselves when they realized that they were all in a Gay bar for similar reasons.

The only thing that hung over Elizabeth like a thunderhead was Jeanette's silence. It had been a week since that night at their house, and Elizabeth felt the silence like a knife blade inside her arms. When her feelings hurt, she actually hurt, physically, had always felt sadness in the little well of flesh between her neck and shoulders and down the soft skin on the inside of her arms. She felt it now as she and Kincaid walked across campus, the conciliation meeting over, the papers signed five minutes ago. Kincaid knew what Elizabeth was thinking about and was determined to change the subject. She couldn't stand it when Elizabeth's arms hurt.

"The truth can definitely smart, can't it? Did you watch Fitzhugh's face? The man was in *pain*."

"Don't gloat, Kincaid. I'm just glad it's relatively over."

"Don't gloat?" Kincaid looked toward an imaginary friend. "We strike a blow for truth, justice and the American Gay, and she says don't gloat." Apparently, her invisible companion was in enthusiastic, though silent, agreement, because Kincaid continued her portion of the dialogue. "I would expect, at the very least, say, a small display of worshipful awe in the face of greatness. A burnt offering, perhaps. One scoop of Baskin-Robbins Rocky Road. *Something* metaphoric." Elizabeth grinned in spite of herself.

Then Kincaid saw Elizabeth's smile fall, her eyes focused beyond Kincaid, the pain coming again, and she followed the line of Elizabeth's gaze to the steps of the building in front of them. Elizabeth stopped dead, heart pounding.

Coming down the steps, Jeanette was watching her feet, moving slowly. She glanced up, saw Elizabeth and froze, then looked hastily away and began to rummage in her briefcase, embarrassment a mask on her face.

Elizabeth's head dropped and Kincaid's eyes filled, afraid to let Jeanette escape, yet certain that she would, that she wanted to. Elizabeth turned toward Kincaid, who watched the two and felt helpless again, connected yet unable to span the distance.

Kincaid looked beyond her and slowly Kincaid's eyes softened and her mouth. Elizabeth stared at the ground and swallowed the sob in her throat. And then a tear fell on something that had been thrust gently in front of her. She wiped her eyes and saw crimson and lavender ribbons, wrapped around the present: Jeanette's worn leather-bound volume of Millay's poetry. Suddenly Jeanette stood next to her, and Elizabeth blinked, relief and surprise spilling from her eyes. She covered Jeanette's hand on the book with her own.

"We have things to discuss, Elizabeth," Jeanette said very, very gently. And she reached out her other hand and cupped Elizabeth's face in her palm.

It had been years since Elizabeth had seen Kincaid's tears.

Only one other soul besides Dog had ever before seen Jeanette's.

TRAVELS WITH DIANA HUNTER
by *Regine Sands*
$8.95

"From the first innocent nuzzle at the 'neck of nirvana' to the final orgasmic fulfillment, Regine Sands stirs us with her verbal foreplay, tongue in cheek humor and tongue in many other places eroticism."

— Jewelle Gomez

JUST HOLD ME
by *Linda Parks*
$7.95

This romantic novel about women loving women, faith and determination will hold you fast in your favorite reading chair from the intriguing beginning to the hope-filled conclusion.

THE LEADING EDGE
edited by *Lady Winston*
introduction by *Pat Califia*
$9.95

THE LEADING EDGE is the hottest, sexiest book yet from Lace's Lady Winston Series. Journey through time from the world of an ancient-day Queen to a 19th century pirate ship skirting the New Orleans shoreline with a bloodthirsty crew of women bent on revenge to lurking the shadows in a modern-day New York bar in search of the perfect candidate to steal away to a forbidding red planet far from Earth. With contributions from Ann Allen Shockley, Dorothy Allison, Jewelle Gomez, Noretta Koertge, Merril Mushroom, Charlotte Stone, Cheryl Clarke, Artemis OakGrove, C. Bailey, Chocolate Waters and others.

JOURNEY TO ZELINDAR
by *Diana Rivers*

$9.95

Sair lived a sheltered life in her city, Eezore. Her father kept her innocent of the world and its wicked ways. When this bright innocent young woman had to marry the captain of the Guard, she had no idea what her fate would be when she refused his marital caresses. Given over to the Guard to preserve her husband's injured pride, Sair was raped and tossed aside to die. JOURNEY TO ZELINDAR is Sair's exciting tale of survival, learning and growth from her rescue by the Hadra women to her eventual telling of her tale to the archivist of Zelindar. Travel with Sair across the Red Line to the powerful mysterious world of the Hadra; learn their secrets and dreams that such a world really exists.

THE RAGING PEACE
Vol. 1 Throne Trilogy
by *Artemis OakGrove*

$7.95

"Dykes on the prowl for nighttime reading, THE RAGING PEACE captivates."

— GCN

DREAMS OF VENGEANCE
Vol. 2. Throne Trilogy
by *Artemis OakGrove*

$7.95

"An overwhelming, breathtaking plot filled with revenge, violence and spiritual turmoil . . . far more than just another SM book."

— KSK

THRONE OF COUNCIL
Vol. 3 Throne Trilogy
by *Artemis OakGrove*

$7.95

". . . concludes the compelling fantasy of a love between two women that withstands the passing of centuries, the barriers of time and memory, reincarnation, earthly trials and spirit war."

— Bookpaper